I0748430

Though One Go with Me

Though One Go with Me

Barry Blackstone

RESOURCE *Publications* • Eugene, Oregon

THOUGH ONE GO WITH ME

Resource Publications
An Imprint of Wipf and Stock Publishers
199 W. 8th Ave., Suite 3
Eugene, OR 97401
www.wipfandstock.com

ISBN 13: 978-1-49825-706-0

Manufactured in the U.S.A.

All scripture quotations, unless otherwise indicated, are taken from the King James Version of the Bible.

I dedicate this series of family adventures
to the Simon family of Kerala, India,
and to their wonderful Christ-like kindness,
and Christian hospitality.

Contents

Prelude

Though One Go with Me

Isaiah 6:8—Also I heard the voice of the Lord, saying, Whom shall I send, and who will go for us? Then said I (Marnie), Here I am; send me.

A desire to revisit India began the moment I returned to Maine in February 2006. (I had sent 40-days teaching and preaching throughout Kerala State and at Kerala Baptist Bible College.) Even in my wildest imagination, I never thought that 'desire' would come to pass within a year, and never did I dream that my daughter Marnie would accompany me on a second adventure to the sub-continent of Asia!

Many, many years ago I wrote a book, "Though Son Go with Me", about my early fishing adventures with my only son Scott. The writing project chronicled Scott's and my angling exploits throughout his boyhood. When I sat down to record my first mission's trip to India, I adapted Scott's title to "Though None Go With Me." The solo trip half-way around the world and back was without a doubt the greatest spiritual ministry mission of my life. Now I am again before my computer screen ready to highlight my return trip to Kerala, and the focus of this journey is very clear to me:

"Though One Go With Me"

To say my daughter Marnie and I have had a wonderful father\daughter relationship her entire life would be an understatement. I wish I could express in poetic prose just how unique our fellowship has been. I know of the theory behind such affection, but our bond has been extra special. It began early because of a birth defect, carried through her infancy, and progressed throughout her childhood and now into adulthood. We have always been able to talk, and our common love for the Lord Jesus Christ and His work only cemented an already cherished connection. Since the age of eight, Marnie's expressed desire has been for overseas missions, and by the time she was 17 she was serving the Lord in Nigeria, West Africa. During her college years she spent a summer in Togo, West Africa, (The adventure that provoked me to write Rendezvous in Paris) and following her graduation from Lancaster Bible College, she joined Crossworld Missions and spent a year in Slovakia in Eastern Europe. It wasn't surprising to me when she said:

"Let's go to India together!"

Marnie had some funds left over from her internship in Bratislava, and I only needed an excuse to return to a land I had fallen in love with.

The opportunity can unexpectedly when the graduation speaker for Kerala Baptist Bible College, scheduled for March 2, 2007, had to back out because of personal reasons. The president of the college (Shibu Simon) contacted me and asked if I was interested. I jumped at the chance, and asked if I could bring someone along. The answer was 'yes', and Marnie and I immediately began to make plans for an India adventure together. Solomon was right when he wrote:

> *Ecclesiastes 4:9—"Two are better than one; because they have a good reward for their labor."*

I had experienced 'delay' before on an overseas mission's trip. My cousin Bob and I were delayed two days before we headed for Australia in the summer of 1972 to do missionary work among the aboriginal people of the Gibson Desert of Western Australia. In the winter of 2007, my daughter and I experienced a four-day delay before heading to India to labor among the Independent Gospel Baptist Churches of Kerala, India. Each delay in my life has left me with the question:

"What did I miss?"

Because of a huge east coast snow storm two days before we were suppose to depart and the confusion that followed, our Delta flight out of Portland, Maine to New York had been cancelled. Despite clear weather on the day of our departure, the 'JetBlue' meltdown at JFK airport had messed up everybody's schedule from Maine to New York City. So our Friday takeoff had to be moved ahead to Tuesday; four days to ponder one of life's most frustrating circumstances: divine delay!

Both Marnie and I took the 'delay' in stride as we traveled back to our home on the coast of Maine to await our new departure date. We had learned long before that all 'starts and stops' of God's people are apart of God's perfect will. It might be frustrating, but our faith still taught us that God is in control of all such delays:

> *Numbers 9:19—"When the cloud tarried long upon the tabernacle . . . then the children of Israel . . . journeyed not."*

As the Good Lord guided the children of Israel though their wilderness journey, He delayed them at times. These divine 'pauses' were for rest, reflection, and recreation. So why were we delayed? What divine purpose could God have had for us?

One of the most famous 'delays' of the Bible is the time that Jesus 'stayed two days longer' (John 11:6) before going to visit His sick friend Lazarus. The only reason given for the procrastination was that the power of God could more vigorously be demonstrated (certainly a resurrection shows greater power than a healing). Was that the reason for Marnie's and my delay to India? What was it that the Lord had to show us? That He was in charge of our itinerary, not the Simon brothers; that He would make the final plans for this trip, not Marnie nor me? We love promptness and things done pronto; whether answers to prayer or travel plans. What I have learned is that God does have appropriate schedules and His delays are always within the boundaries of His greater purpose for our lives.

From the very first moment of our India trip together, Marnie and I were reminded of who was in control of this endeavor. We would experience no other 'delays' on the trip, for God had made things perfectly clear in the first four-days!

"Though One Go With Me" is a collection of spiritual blessings and lessons Marnie and I received on our 2007 trip to Kerala together. It is my prayer and hope these remembrances will help you in your journey with Christ though all delays and departures and days.

Barry Blackstone
March 15, 2007

1

God's Ordered Steps

Psalms 37:23—The steps of a good man (woman) are ordered by the Lord; and He delighteth in his (her) way.

DESPITE THE feeling of disappointment over our four-day delay, Marnie and I were not discouraged over our 'false' start. This attitude had developed over the years during numerous situations that the Good Lord had put us through. No matter how many times the Lord allows delay, one only needs too look around for a hidden blessing, or two.

We serve the God of 'all blessings' (Ephesians 1:3). For me it was simply the blessing of sharing this India experience with my daughter. I had put her on planes for Nigeria, Togo, Slovakia, and many other destinations alone. Now I was going with her, or maybe, she was going with me. The very first blessing of this adventure was being with Marnie. We had served the Lord together, and had been co-laborers together with Christ in diverse ministries over our 27 years together. From singing together in the church choir to working side by side together in AWANA, (a youth ministry) Marnie and I had experienced the joys and pleasures of ministering together for the cause of Christ. In all those years we had only left the United States once to labor for the Lord abroad. Marnie was only seven at the time, but we experienced the blessing of serving in the same summer camp in Canada. If you think that Marnie was just a camper; it was on that trip Marnie lead her very first person to her Lord and Savior Jesus Christ. (Marnie had herself accepted the Lord as her Savior at 3 1\2 years of age!)

Spiritual blessings can come in various forms and many are missed or overlooked if one doesn't keep his or her eyes open for them. Four-days after our scheduled flight from Maine to New York had been cancelled; Marnie and I were on another Delta flight to JFK Airport. This time there were no delays (a blessing), but we were facing another dilemma according to our travel agent. Because Delta Airlines had no working arrangements with Kuwait Air, we were warned that we might have to pay a rescheduling fee because we had missed the Kuwait flight that Friday before! We were told we needed to go to the Kuwait Air service desk once we had arrived at JFK and probably would have to pay a $150 fee.

One of the great blessings of India the first time around was the impact a few American dollars had in Kerala. If we had to pay this rescheduling fee that would mean one hundred and fifty fewer dollars for India. On the way through the massive New York airport, we prayed that there would be 'no charge' for our change of plans. Marnie boldly approached the counter and spoke directly to a middle age, Middle Eastern man, and within a few minutes, after looking over our papers, he said, "I don't know why they sent you here; there will be no further charges!" To some this blessing would have passed them by, but for Marnie and me we were praising the Lord for His blessing of 'no further cost'; truly, the steps of God's children are ordered of the Lord and along the way: what blessings!

Each time I head out on an extended journey, I marvel at the orderliness of the world I now live in. After reading and hearing of the difficult trips of the early missionaries to places like India, I stand amazed just how easy it now is to travel from Ellsworth, Maine to Edyappara, India. Some of the steps my daughter and I took were planned, but once we touched down in India: God's orderly steps became very clear, and what blessings.

Ellsworth, Portland, New York, London, Kuwait City, and Trivandrum were all stops as we traveled a day and a half to the fabled land of India. Once we touched down the plans of our human travel agent ended, and the hand of the Lord took over through the presence of the 'boys': Shibu, Shaju, and Binu. Waiting at the Trivandrum Airport at 4:30 AM were my dear friends from my first trip in 2006. They had traveled from their home village of Edyappara the day before to be in Trivandrum to meet our plane. Within minutes of leaving customs, we were driven into the city to freshen up at the MoonStar Motel, India's version of Motel 6. From a fourth floor balcony Marnie experienced her first India sunrise and our first 100 degree plus day (we had 13 more just like it ahead of us) had started.

Our first stop was to meet Sam, the newest member of the Simon family (Sheena and Joe's new baby boy). Sam was a visible answer to prayer. When I left India the year before one of the prayer requests I had returned with was for Sheena and Joe to have a family. Married 12 years, they had not as yet been blessed with children; a highly regarded event in Indian society. We rejoiced with them over their 'Isaac' in their new home, Melita. (Indian families like to name their houses. Melita is an island in the Mediterranean Sea which means 'refuge.' Marnie and I found it so during our visit, another blessing.)

Our next stop was to visit Pastor T P Sachai at the Ooruttambalam Baptist Church, the church Marnie and I was scheduled to be at on our original first day in India. We got to see the church building and meet Sachai's wife and have fellowship in their home. Their son Liben was one of my students the year before at KBBC; another small piece to the massive puzzle that is Kerala had now been put into place. What a joy it has been to put that spiritual puzzle together through the ordered steps and blessings of the Lord, and now with the companionship of my daughter to help: another huge blessing.

We headed north after Ooruttambalam to Puthur were the Gospel Team of the mission had been laboring for a number of months. Another unexpected side trip to meet old friends from the year before; actually on the front line of hopefully a new church plant in Kerala (number 20?). I had a prayer for them, and to actually see them at their work were steps I didn't know I would get to walk. Both Marnie and I challenged them and received from them a typical Indian response of hospitality and honor. Among the group was another one of my students (Shaji Matthew) from KBBC, now working for the IGBC. Oh, how sweet and blessed are the ordered steps of the Lord!

2

American Professor Returns

Acts 21:6— . . . And they returned home again.

AFTER A short stop and a quick meal (you never make a stop in India without something to eat) to revisit Julie's (Shibu's wife) parents (Daisy and Paul) and to introduce them to my daughter, we pressed on toward Kangazha and a glorious homecoming!

I had only spent 40-days in Edyappara, but that time cemented in my heart and the hearts of the people of Kangazha Church and Kerala Baptist Bible College a hometown relationship. I was treated like the honored guest returning, and now I had come 'home' with my daughter. Whether the Simon family, or the students and staff at KBBC, the welcome was just as I expected it to be: friendly, gracious, and loving. Many had thought, as I had imagined, that our time apart would be long, but now we were in each other's presence in just twelve short months. With open arms and broad smiles, I was greeted as an old friend returning 'home' from the far country.

Can a distant place, a strange land feel like home? Can a different people with a strange speech sound like home? Can a hot climate, a tropical paradise seem like home? For me, the answer to all those questions is 'yes'! I did find a 'home' away from home a year before, and my return was simply that: a homecoming! To the students of KBBC their American professor had come back; to the teachers of Kerala Baptist Bible College their colleague had returned, and to the pastors of the Kerala churches their brother had reappeared. The joy on their lips and the sparkle in their eyes brought a smile to my face. It wasn't long however before their attention to me switched to my daughter. Marnie would soon be the 'star', as I was the year before. Her red-hair and pink skin stood out in the brown faces and black hair of the Malayalam people. Her height brought her above the crowd, and her friendly nature was an instant hit. These people were the very medicine I had hoped they would be for Marnie. (More later)

One of the reasons I believe in 'a taste of heaven' on earth is the experiences I have had in India. Heaven is a distant place. Heaven is a place were people wait for visits from those they love. Heaven is also home. I have yet to experience Heaven, but I believe I have experienced the thrill that makes Heaven: heavenly; a welcoming crowd of brothers and sisters just waiting a glimpse of your coming. As Marnie and I made the rounds on that first evening in Edyappara, the children glowed and the adults bowed. We were welcomed in a formal service at the Kangazha Church, and were treated as a brother and a sister to all. If I never get another chance to return, I will carry around with me for the rest of my days the soul-stirring thrill of knowing what it really feels like to be the honored professor and pastor returning from afar. Could Heaven be any better than that, certainly, but for now India will do!

One of the first realities that confronted my daughter on our first day in India was the extreme temperatures. After one morning in the heat that was Kerala, Marnie realized that the cloths she had brought along for this trip were just to hot to be comfortable. It was then I decided to take my daughter on an Indian cloth shopping spree.

One of the unique aspects of this trip to India was the fact that we were going to travel to India on Marnie's 27th birthday (February 17) and return from India on my 56th birthday (March 6). The first part of that plan fell through during our 4-day delay. Marnie was originally going to celebrate her birthday with me in Kuwait City, but the Good Lord had overruled (perhaps, in answer to her mother's prayer), and she celebrated at our home on the coast of Maine. One of the birthday gifts I was going to give her on the trip was some Indian cloths. Despite the divine delay, the shopping trip happened within 24-hours after our arrival in Edyappara.

For this very special birthday present I enlisted the help of Julie Simon and Reneeshya Ariachacil, the college librarian. What does an American preacher know about Indian women's clothing? I haven't bought American cloths for my American wife in 25 years, so why would I try to buy my daughter cloths in India? Julie told me she knew of a perfect clothing store about five miles from Edyappara. So after chapel at KBBC, where both Marnie and I got a chance to speak, we were off for the Star Wedding Centre in the village of Karukachal. On the way we stopped into the bank at Parrathanam where I got 43.75 rupees for every American greenback. Once again I felt like a rich man as my wallet was filled with scores of 500 and 1000 rupee bills!

The clothing and cloth store was located on the second floor of a two-story complex in downtown Karukachal. The streets were crowded with shoppers as we parked behind the building and walked through a back alley to the front of the store. When we walked into the air-conditioned (which was very nice and very rare) clothing store, we discovered that we were the only customers. For the next hour, the girls (Shibu and I sat and talked to the store manager) looked at churidhars (an Indian pant-suit) and sarees (the formal Indian dress). At one time I counted seven clerks waiting on my daughter. The only regret was that my dear wife wasn't there to experience this birthday shopping spree with her beloved Marnie. Coleen would have loved it, the shopper that she is. When it was over Marnie had picked out four churidhars of various colors, and a beautiful chiffon sari to wear to graduation. We also bought a piece of fabric to make a blouse for the sari, and on our way home we stopped at a tailor shop for a fitting. The lady at the shop promised that she would have it done before graduation. As I watched my daughter trying on cloths, all I could think of was what Solomon said of his virtuous woman:

> She maketh herself coverings of tapestry; her clothing is silk and purple (orange). (Proverbs 31:22)

The first time Marnie walked out into the lanes of Edyappara in one of her new Indian outfits, the people remarked how this American professor had brought an Indian princess with him!

3

Teaching Indians to Fish

I Timothy 3:2—A bishop then must be . . .
apt to teach.

When one desires to go fishing in a strange body of water, it is important to pick wisely your fishing guide. The same is true with spiritual fishing:

> And Jesus, walking by the sea of Galilee, saw two brethren, Simon called Peter, and Andrew his brother, casting a net into the sea: for they were fishers. (Matthew 4:18)

As Jesus got ready to cast off into the fishing grounds of Galilee, he picked two brothers to join Him. I also chose two brothers to fish with when I went to India in 2006. As I returned with Marnie in 2007, I was excited to fish again with the Simon brothers.

Thakadiel Sackson Simon (Shibu) and Shaju Simon Thakadiel's grandfather Sachai (Zacchaeus) had been converted in the 1930's through the work of English missionaries. There father, Thakadiel Simon, was born in 1942. Thakadiel's father, an evangelist, led him to Christ and in 1966 he surrendered his life to full-time Christian service. Thakadiel received his Bachelor of Science degree from the

University of Kerala in 1964 and his master of Divinity from Faith Theological Seminary, near Philadelphia, Pennsylvania in 1971. Starting with a gift of $70 from a church in upper State New York, Simon returned to his hometown (Edyappara) in Kangazha in 1973 and started a local Baptist church. Over the next thirty years the work multiplied to the 19 churches of the Independent Gospel Baptist Churches, the Associated Missions of India, the Mercy Children's Christian Home, the Bethany Christian English Medium Day School, and the Kerala Baptist Bible College.

With a staff of over 100 people: the churches, mission outreaches, orphanage, day school, and college have been reaching into the State of Kerala with the Gospel of Christ and to many other Indian States. Covering a population of over 35 million people, Kerala is one of the strongest Christian states in all of India today; in part, because of the faithful spiritual fishing of Thakadiel and his dear wife Annamma. Then on January 8, 2003, with the sudden home going of Thakadiel Simon, the burden of the extensive Indian work fell on the shoulders of Thakadiel's two sons: Shibu (35 years old) and Shaju (30 years old). Shibu took on the responsibility of the American fund raising aspect of the mission through their United States mission board: Partners in Evangelism International, and Shaju took over the directorship of the daily operation of the mission in India. With a well trained staff already in place, and with pastors and evangelists and missionaries already laboring, the work has progressed despite the unexpected departure of the founder and spiritual leader of the work.

After my first trip to India, I knew that I had chosen well my fishing partners for the great fishing hole that is

India (over a billion souls now). Like Jesus of old, I simply borrowed the Simon's boat to cast out into the spiritual 'deep' (Luke 5:4) that is India. It was nice to get my daughter involved in the spiritual 'draught', and what a spiritual 'haul' is possible. I had come to fish, but also to teach others how to be 'fishers-of-men'!

I have always loved teaching. Ever since my high school history teacher, Mrs. Cole, allowed me to teach my high school senior class about World War Two, I have gotten great satisfaction out of instructing anyone about anything. As I taught at Kerala Baptist Bible College the year before, I experienced first hand the joys of being a college professor. To return to the campus and to see my students again was my first priority on my second trip.

I have also loved to take people fishing; to show them where and how to catch fish. One of the joys of visiting India was to teach another generation how to fish for men. Jesus was a great teacher and an even greater 'fisher-of-men.' I have been a serious student of both for over forty years now. Like fishing for fish, fishing for men also has a number of proven Biblical techniques. It was with great satisfaction that I was able to pass on these tactics to the students of KBBC. I was excited to return and to hear how their fishing year had been.

It wasn't long after I arrived at KBBC that I learned that some of the best teaching time I would have with the students wasn't in class, but out of class and in their chapel services. Because I lived next door to the campus, it was my daily routine, class day, or no class day, to walk over to the college and talk with whosoever was around. I continued this practice on my second trip. Besides walking pass the orphanage everyday, I also walked to KBBC everyday. Sometimes I would talk with the boys washing the dishes after a noon meal, and at other time I would talk to them as they cleaned up in the morning by the 'cement pond' (every building had a concrete holding tank for water). I loved to walk with the boys and girls that took evening classes back to their dorms. It was then we talked of home and homeland and how to catch the souls of men either in Assam or America. It was their I meet and fell in love with the fishermen that where preparing their lives for the great spiritual hauls in Orissa, Kerala, Assam, Chhattisgarh, Karnataka, Tamil Nadu, Andhra Pradesh, and Nagaland.

It was not long after I started to instruct these young people that I began to realize the gigantic obstacles facing these future pastors and evangelists and missionaries. My Maine brogue was strange to them, but they held onto every word I spoke like it came from Jesus Himself. Their respect for me was beyond honor, and I was humbled by their desire to learn of me. I had never found the same attitude in American young people (the only exception has been my daughter), even though I have been a youth worker for most of my ministry. Time would fail me to share with you all the personal experiences this pastor, turned professor, had with the students of KBBC over these past two years. As I write this, the student body of KBBC comes from six different states of India, and I have had a very small part to play in the 'bringing-in' of souls in India, but I am proud to say I have at least had a small part in the catch, for as I was instructing them they were teaching me. (As I put this book project to bed, I have just returned from my 3rd trip to India. On this trip I got the chance to ministry in Andhra Pradesh for a week. In a six day, eleven meeting crusade 54 people made a profession of faith; the most I have seen in any one period of time in my entire ministry. My co-laborers in India have also shown me how to fish!)

4

Spice Necklaces at 504 Colony

Revelation 21:5— . . . I made all things new . . .

WITHIN 24 hours of our arrival in Kangazha, Marnie and I were on the road to 504 Colony (the fifteenth church of the IGBC I had visited) and to one of the early church plants of the ministry. This was an area in which the Indian government had given land for colonization (why the name). Brother Simon had started a church there in the 1980s, and it was still proclaiming the Gospel of Christ.

I had thought that I had experienced everything on my first trip to India in 2006, but the people of Kerala always seemed to have a pleasant surprise for me just when I thought I had seen it all! Pastor KJ Thomas and his flock greeted us warmly. A traditional Malayalam greeting involves the placing of a colorful myla around a visitor's neck. By the time Marnie and I got to 504 Colony, we had already received a dozen of the artificial flower necklaces. We were not surprised when the pastor wanted to officially welcome us at the beginning of the service; what surprised and pleased us was the kind of myla they placed around our necks.

As my daughter and I bowed before the representatives of the Baptist Church of 504 Colony, they placed a stringer of black pepper necklaces over our heads. Black pepper was one of the very first widely used spices for seasoning food. When the 'black gold' was discovered by western explorers in India, a very profitable trade developed between Europe and India. Just before I went to India, I was reading a book about the early explorers and what motivated them to risk death on the open seas. Because pepper was so expensive in Europe by the time of the Middle Ages (the only source was an overland route controlled by the Arabs), it was partly responsible for the Portuguese discovering a sea route to India by way of the Cape of Good Hope, South Africa.

One of the spices Marnie and I (Ezekiel 27:22) would learn about while in India was black pepper, and here we had a necklace of the famous spice placed around our necks as a welcome gift. Native to India, black pepper is obtained chiefly from a small climbing shrub. It is grown all over tropical Asia today, but Marnie and I had a chance to see where the plant was originally planted by the Good Lord Himself. The berry is red when it is gathered, and turns black as it dries. We soon learned that we were in pepper country in 504 Colony and that this special greeting was the people's way of welcoming us to their part of Kerala. Those two pepper necklaces found a place in our return baggage to Maine, and they have found a place on a shelf in my office to this day!

Each peppercorn had been pierced with a needle and strung on a black piece of thread. How much time it had taken to do this I know not, but up until that time it was the most meaningful myla that I had been presented. It was a special treat for Marnie, seeing she is a cook and one of her desires in India was to gather native spices. Little did she know that she would be wearing the world's most famous spice around her neck. We didn't even have to go to the market to get our first spice; all we had to do was to visit an isolated church in a backwater area of central Kerala. God's spices are sweetest when you follow His leading.

Once the pepper myla was presented Marnie gave her testimony, and I shared a message based on this question:

Are there new things in Christ we don't have to wait until we get to Heaven for?

I shared these three thoughts:

1. *A New Life*. Romans 6:4. Most of us know of II Corinthians 5:17 and the 'new creature.' I believe the 'new creature' is the new life, 'the newness of life.' If you have experienced this then you know of what I speak (Romans 7:6). From the oldness to the newness; our attitude changes, our goals change, our motivations change, our priorities change, our desires change, and our habits change. Born again is the great phrase to describe this change because when we come to know Christ it is as if we start life anew, fresh; just like a new experience in India with pepper!
2. *A New Living*. I Peter 2:2. Everything is new to a baby. Remember recording your child's first taste of solid food, their first steps, that first trip; how wide-eyed they were? Why, because everything they saw and touched was new to them. So it is with the new Christian: a new fellowship begins, new friends, a

new food (the Bible-Hebrews 10:20). A new and living way has begun for them, and all things become 'new'! They have a new way of acting, talking, thinking (Romans 12:2) as their mind is reNEWed. This all happens because of the teaching in II Corinthians 10:5 and Philippians 4:8. Now there is a new way of seeing things, a new way of living; even if that something new is something old: like pepper.

3. *A New Lifestyle.* Hebrews 12:24. Our newness in style is based on a new covenant, a new testament, a new promise between us and God (Colossians 3:10). The new man is based on a reNEWed knowledge, a new lump (I Corinthians 5:7) that can be molded and fashioned by the Spirit of God, and that new lifestyle can be lived here (Titus 2:12), not just there! Most are waiting for the new heaven and the new earth (Revelation 21:1) to live the new life, the new living, the new lifestyle, but we don't have to wait! Has anything new happened to you lately? Marnie and I had experienced in 504 Colony a new understanding of pepper, but have you come to a new understanding of God and His Son Jesus Christ?

Recently, the Lord has given to me an insight into Isaiah 43:19: 'a new thing.' I believe I know what that new thing is for me, but what is it for you? I have come to believe that we have a lot of 'newness' here on this planet (II Corinthians 2:9), but we must look for it (Isaiah 48:6). It is time we enjoy now the new things in Christ, and not wait for 'all things to become new'! I learned this from a simple stringer of peppercorn.

5

Inroads into a Heathen Land

Psalms 2:8—Ask me, and I shall give thee the heathen for thine inheritance, and the uttermost parts of the earth for thy possession.

Before Marnie and I left for India, I got this update from Shibu Simon about a potential problem developing near Kerala Baptist Bible College. He wrote:

> Many of you have heard about the land situation near the Bible College in Kerala. Our Hindu neighbors who lived there for many years sold the land to a Muslim organization without saying a word to us. We have been in great fellowship with this family although they are not believers. This move surprised us and shocked us. And to know this sale could potentially pose some threats to us in the future discouraged us. We prayed. Many of you hearing the news prayed with us. From the managing trustee of this organization, we have learned that they are going to build a mosque and a place to house and train young boys! We told him that since we live so close to the property and the college is located a few feet from there, we could really use it and that he should sell it

> to us. First, he said no and promised us that he would build high walls around the property so that it will not cause an inconvenience to us. We pressed more and prayed more. Finally, before all other trustees of this organization had a chance to meet, the man sold it to us saying, 'I believe God really wants you to have this property and I do not wish to hold on to it another day.' Praise God! He can melt the mind of a man and provide for His own.

Having read this before we left for Kerala little did Marnie and I know we would have a part to play in this great answer to prayer.

Within days of our arrival, Marnie and I were asked to join a number of the members of the mission team to the newly purchased land told about in the mission letter above. The mission had just been given the key to the small building on that property. We were asked to lead a prayer and praise meeting to the reclaiming of this heathen property for the Cause of Christ. As the front door was unlocked, the first thing that caught our eye was the pictures of some Hindu gods on the wall. As a matter of fact, the only articles left behind by the former owner were these pictures of his gods. After a season of singing praises unto the Almighty and prayers of thanksgiving and dedication to His Son, we tore the pictures from the walls. In my heart the Lord reminded me of the verse I have printed at the beginning of this remembrance. Marnie and I had the privilege of participating in repossessing a small piece of heathen land in an 'uttermost part of the earth.' How many of us get such an opportunity? As for me, it was one of the top ten blessings of my 'Though One Go With Me ' trip to India, but the blessings of that day were not over.

Within minutes Marnie and I had walked over to KBBC to share in their daily chapel service. On my first trip I had been able to share with the students and staff of KBBC 14 times. In my first meeting with the people of KBBC, I wanted to bring a connection to the experience I had just had with the daunting task before them to reclaim more of their heathen country for Christ. It was a gigantic goal, but giants are for slaying, are they not? Marnie and I sang Philip Bliss's classic church hymn 'Dare to Be a Daniel', and I decided to share with them the five characteristics of a 'giant-killer.' ("Many giants great and tall stacking through the land, headlong to the earth will fall when meet by Daniel's band.") Giants are not always huge warriors, as with Goliath. They can be religions like Hindu or Islam. Using David's fine example I shared this with them:

1. *Be Obedient*. I Samuel 17:17–20. The father said it, and David did it. David was so use to obeying his earthly father that when his heavenly Father spoke he obeyed (Ephesians 6:1). Giant-killers are made, not born. Our basic nature is to disobey just like our first parents, but a child that is taught to obey will eventually obey father, or Father! Even when the order is to go up against a fearful giant like Islam.

2. *Be Responsible*. I Samuel 17:17–20. Before David left for the battle front, he made sure the sheep, his first charge, were taken care of: 'he left the sheep with a keeper.' Some people think that a new mission relieves them of their current responsibilities.

Not so! If we show responsibility in one area, God will give us responsibility in another mission. This is Jesus' teaching in the parable of the talents (Matthew 25:14–30). Faithfulness in Edyappara over a small piece of land, might lead to a greater conquest in the land of Assam.

3. *Be Faithful.* I Samuel 17:34–35. David was faithful in defending his flock from an Asiatic bear, a very aggressive creature, and an Asiatic lion, the original king of beasts, so this set the stage for his willingness to defend the Army of the Living God against Goliath. (I Corinthians 4:2) Faithfulness is a key ingredient in giant-killers whether in private contests, as David experienced in the hills outside Bethlehem, or in public contests, as David would prove in his battle with Goliath in the Valley of Elah (Luke 19:17). Little battles, no matter how difficult, are only training exercises for the big battles with giants throughout the land of India!

4. *Be Yourself.* I Samuel 17:39. Can you picture a man's armor on a boy's body? David was smart enough to know that he was no expert in the traditional weapons of war, but his confidence was in the sling and stone (Matthew 6:27). Whether bears or lions or giants, the foe might change but our weapons must stay the same. Oh, there would come a day when David would fight with sword and spear, but on this day he would be himself and fight with what he knew. I am convinced that many Christians have given up using the Bible to quote some philosopher instead of using

their primary weapon: the Word of God. Use what works and stay with it. God created you to be you, not Billy Graham, or King Saul. You're enough with God on your side, for you and God make a majority in any situation or circumstance in Kerala, or beyond.

5. *Be Trusting.* I Samuel 17:40. All of Saul's army saw Goliath to big to fight, while David saw Goliath as to big to miss! Why? It all came down to 'Who' David trusted. Courage comes with confidence, and David's confidence was in the Lord (I Samuel 17:47), as can be our confidence and trust in Edyappara, your town, or Ellsworth, my town.

As Shibu and his fellow ministers trusted that God would work out the situation with the land, so too will God help us through the giant obstacles and gigantic roadblocks that we will face. It was such a blessing to have apart in the preparing of a group of future 'giant-killers.'

6

A Christmas to Remember

James 1:27—Pure religion and undefiled before God and the Father is this, to visit the fatherless . . . in their affliction . . .

"WHERE IS Marnie?" This is the question that was on the lips of every orphan at the Mercy Christian Children's Home. Despite the fact that we had barely been in India 48-hours, the children of Edyappara had already fallen in love with my daughter. Marnie has always been a 'child' magnet. Her years of teaching Sunday school, AWANA, working with Child Evangelism Fellowship, and her two trips to Africa working with children had resulted in an instant love affair with any child that comes within her sight. The God-given gift is that every child she contacts seems to have the same attraction. We had visited the orphanage of Edyappara within minutes of our arrivals, and so by the time I walked over early that first Saturday in India without Marnie, the children wanted to know where Marnie was?

After a late night traveling the rough (Marnie said she hadn't seen rougher roads since her days in Nigeria) forty miles back from 504 Colony, Marnie had slept in that morning. One of the joys I discovered during my first trip to Kerala was early morning walks just before sunrise. The air was cooler and the activity of early morning in a rural Indian village was fascinating to watch. This trip I found the heat more oppressive, but the village and villagers were still worth the sweat you had to endure. The children at the orphanage were always the best part of the walk.

During my first visit to Edyappara, I tried every day to make a trip over to see the 'fatherless.' My schedule was such that I had plenty of time to minister in this way. Our schedule this time was much more involved, so each trip had to count. I learned very quickly that a trip to the orphanage was not the same alone as it was with Marnie. Oh, the kids still loved to see me and the candy I usually passed out did bring a sweet taste to our relationship, but Marnie had brought something with her that gave the children a little extra thrill: that is besides her red-hair!

Before Marnie and I headed off to India, Karen Bowden, a lady in our Church in Ellsworth, offered to loan Marnie her new digital camera for the trip. With a powerful zoom and the capacity of taking 700 pictures on a single photo card, it was ideal for what Marnie wanted to do. Marnie loves taking pictures and turning those photographs into scrapbooks and photo albums. As I returned to get Marnie after my morning walk, she decided that this might be a perfect time to fulfill one of her goals for the trip. Marnie wanted to take a portrait photograph of each of the orphans to give to the people that had helped her create a special Christmas for each of the 'fatherless' of Mercy Home. With Karen's camera, Marnie was able to do this and to show each child their shining, smiling faces after the picture was taken. This is what they loved best about Marnie, and of course, the hug after each picture!

One of the reasons Marnie had an instant connection with the orphans at the Edyappara orphanage was the 'Christmas Child' project she has spearheaded the summer before her first trip to India. Following my trip in 2006, Marnie had challenged our church to provide a Christmas for the orphans I had meet on my first trip. Throughout that summer, Marnie collected clothing and gifts for each of the 24 orphans at the home. When the collection was over we had five large boxes full of pants, shorts, T-shirts, socks, skirts, dresses, sweaters, light jackets, towels, wash cloths, crayons, stickers, balls, coloring books, hair clips, candy, markers, toy cars, bracelets, and just about everyone placed a picture of their family in the special bags. Marnie had run the project on the bases of each family in our church adopting an individual child. I had come home with their names, but no individual pictures.

One of the first joys Marnie and I received when I took her to the home that first day in Kerala were the kids coming out of their rooms holding up the pictures of the people who had sent them their Christmas package. It was then we heard for the first time the great excitement that took place at the Mercy Christian Children's Home on December 25, 2006.

Marnie and I had shipped five boxes of presents on September 26–27. The first three boxes didn't arrive until November 30! When Shibu Simon got the boxes he didn't tell the kids anything about the special presents that had arrived from the Emmanuel Baptist Church. By the time December 25 had come, the other two boxes had also arrived. The day before Christmas Shibu told the kids that special packages had come for them from America. As Shibu told us the Christmas story, we learned that this was the first time in the history of the orphanage that anybody had done anything like this for the kids. Our joy was overwhelming as Shibu described the excitement of the kids and the sheer pleasure they got when he presented to each of the 'fatherless' their bag full of cloths and toys and other things. They couldn't imagine that they each had their own package! Shibu said that as the gifts were opened the children kept asking him if these presents were all for them? Shibu said it was one of the best experiences he had ever witnessed in his ministry in Edyappara.

Now it was our joy to rejoice with these special kids as Marnie one by one took their pictures for the individuals and families who had given a special Christmas to the orphans of Edyappara. Marnie's photographs of these children will forever put a face to the "Christmas Children of Kerela!

7

A Sunday Safari to the Summit

Ezekiel 43:12— . . . upon the top of the mountain the whole limit thereof about shall be holy . . .

One of my desires for my daughter Marnie on our 2007 India trip was to take her into the mountains of Eastern Kerala. I had been taken on an Indian safari as a treat for my month long ministry at Kerala Baptist Bible College the year before and the blessings were beyond description. (You can read all about them in my first book, Though None Go with Me.) It was by far the most pleasant personal day I had in my first Indian experience. I wanted Marnie to see the massive hills and deep gorges along the KK Road (Kottayam to Kumily) to Tamil Nadu. I also wanted her to witness the patchwork quilt that is the tea plantations of mountainous Kerala. I finally wanted her to enjoy the cooler air and refreshing showers that happen at 10,000 feet; a pleasant relief from the oppressive heat of tropical Kangazha. Our first Sunday in India fulfilled all these desires and so many, many more.

Our Sabbath safari started very early on February 25, 2007. We were up at 5:20 AM for a 6:00 AM departure for a Sunday morning service at the Koch Kamakshi Baptist

Church; just 74 miles away (the 10:30 AM service would be starting before we arrived). The trip from Kangazha to Koch Kamakshi was a slow, winding climb through 'dead men' curves and hairpin turns; all the while steadily climbing upward. The autumn before our trip my wife and I took Marnie on her first climb up Mount Washington in the White Mountains of New Hampshire. I have a picture in my India journal of Marnie and I standing at the top of New England's highest peak (6288 feet); our climb to Koch took us over 4000 feet higher. As with my first climb, Marnie was taken back by the amazing sights along the mountainous path.

I had placed Marnie in the front seat beside our driver, Binu. Besides us, the Simon 'boys' had come along, as well as their mother, Annamma. We stopped along the way to take a picture or two, and to enjoy the air that was dramatically cooler than what we had experienced in our first 72-hours in India. The climb took us nearly three hours. Despite the fact this was the best road in the region; the accent was still slow given the twisting highway and the busy traffic. We did have to stop for some Diesel (I noted in my journal that we bought 34.21 liters (7.5 gallons) for 1026.30 rupees ($25.65) at K E Scariah and Company, a gas station of India Oil) before making the summit around mid-morning.

After mile after mile of rocky outcroppings and mile after mile of dangerous drop offs, we reached the plateau and turned left on the Kumily Road. It was in that last thousand feet we began to see the rolling mountaintops covered in tea bushes. The season of picking tea was over, but the well groomed tea plants were amazingly neat. It is a sight beyond imagination: on that summit of an India mountain range is a vista that will take your breath away for its sheer beauty!

After a quick stop for breakfast at the Edassery Resort in Kattappana, we hurried along the Kumily Road to Koch Kamakshi. The church service at one of the oldest church plants of IGBC (Independent Gospel Baptist Churches of India) was just beginning. Despite the fact that we were running a bit late, Shibu still allowed Marnie and me to stop a couple of times along the way to get a picture of us in the tea bushes and standing beside the coffee trees.

One of the differences between my first visit to the summit and my second trip was the coffee trees were in full bloom and the smell was divine. I am not a coffee drinker, but I must admit one of the greatest smells I have ever experienced in my life is the aroma of budding coffee trees. Almost from the moment we made the summit, this wonderful scent could be inhaled. Both Marnie and I asked, "What is that marvelous smell?" I had heard of the 'spice winds', but now I understand exactly what they are. The sights and smells of Koch were very distracting as we came near the 'red-brick' Baptist church of Pastor Matthewkutty.

Unlike most of the churches in the confederation, we had to walk down to this simple sanctuary. The people had already begun to sing their haunting Malayalam hymns as we made our way into their presence. We were greeted with honor and hospitality. This would be the 16th of the 19 churches I had now visited in the group. With prayers and singing (including: The Sweet By and By and More about Jesus), the service flowed as the folks slowly filled the building. Marnie shared her testimony from Hebrews 12:2 and I shared a message called "God Sent His Son." When I sat down Pastor Matthewkutty asked for testimonies: 19

people stood and thanked the Good Lord for His wonderful blessings. The service ended a little after 1 o'clock!

Following the meeting, we had a great time of fellowship including taking pictures with the congregation, and receiving a variety of spices that grew wild around the church building. Once again Marnie was the center of attraction as both young and old gathered around my daughter to ask questions and to get their picture taken with her. Most of these activities took place outside, that is, until it began to rain. In my first trip to India it only rained three times in 40 days. This would be the only rain we experienced on this trip. It rained hard for about an hour only cooling down the air even more. While it rained we had lunch with the pastor and his family in the sanctuary, and talked of the blessings of the day. The beating of the rain on the tile roof only added to the joy of the fellowship. All I could think about was that classic church hymn, "There shall be showers of blessing, O that today they might fall", and falling they were all around us!

8

Sermon at Thopramkudy

Hebrews 10:25—Not forsaking the assembling of ourselves together, as the manner of some is; but exhorting one another: and so much the more, as ye see the day approaching.

IT WAS only 13 miles between the two most easterly churches in the IGBC; our next stop was at Thopramkudy in Marnie's and my Sabbath day safari into the mountains of Eastern Kerala. We left Koch Kamakshi around 3 PM with a heart full of blessings and a treasure chest full of spices. While we waited for the afternoon shower to pass, the people kept bringing us samples of the local spices; picked from the plants and bushes and trees around the church. We left with a bag full of vanilla, cardamom, pepper, coffee, and cumin.

We arrived in Thopramkudy at the height of a Roman Catholic festival. I had discovered on my first trip that there is very little difference between a Hindu celebration and a Christian festival. The streets reminded me of the activity at the Fryeburg Fair (the best known country fair in Maine). It had a carnival atmosphere with plenty of food to eat and more loud music than one could stand. During our worship service at the church, we could hear clearly the music being played downtown; despite the fact we were a mile or more out of town and on the backside of a hill!

We were warmly welcomed by Pastor P M Chacko and his church family. The group was small because of the time of the service. Most churches in India don't have an evening service because of the distances the people have to travel, yet nearly thirty people had hung around all afternoon to fellowship with Marnie and me and the Simon family. Each and every time I participated in a Kerala worship service I am struck by the sacrifice these people make to worship together. Most, if not all, have to walk to church in terrible heat or rain; depending on the season, yet they are there. Few 'forsake the assembly of themselves together', as the manner of most American Christians. The people covet and cherish their times together, as demonstrated by the believers of Thompramkudy on that memorable Sunday in the mountains of Kerala.

After a few songs and a few prayers, Marnie once again shared her testimony using I Peter 1:25. I followed with this message, "The Four Stages of the Christian's Life":

1. Stage One-Without Christ. Romans 3:23. This is where every Christian ultimately starts (John 1:13). I was born into a Christian family, a Christian Church, a Christian country, but I myself was not a Christian at the time (Titus 3:3). I was lost, dead, and spiritually alone (Romans 3:10–18). Even the Harry Ironsides and the Billy Sundays started here, and until we find this place we have no hope.

2. Stage Two-In Christ. Acts 16:31. 'One door and only one and yet its sides are two, inside and outside on which side are you?' We start 'outside', this is stage one, but if we move into stage two, we come 'inside' (John 1:12 and Titus 3:4–6). Salvation results in our being in Him and He in us (Galatians 2:20). 'Things are different now something happened to me when I gave my heart to Jesus!' (II Corinthians 5:17) Everything changes, but the greatest change is what happens next, or should happen next. There are many who believe that stage two is the last stage: to their lose!

3. Stage Three-For Christ. Romans 12:1. So many take Christ and then go their own way. The Life of the Christian ought to be 'for Christ.' In service 'for Him' (I Corinthians 6:20). Is not this the lesson of Jesus' encounter with Peter (John 21:15–17)? You have made Him Saviour of your soul, but have not made Him Lord of your Life? There are so many that have not advanced into stage three, and the tragic result for the Christian and for Christianity has been terrible. The Scripture is every clear on this matter; we are to work 'for' Him, and live 'for' Him!

4. Stage Four-With Christ. Revelations 14:13 and Psalms 116:15. In the biography of Harry Ironside this outlines was used by Harry to preach Billy Sunday's funeral. The point that Harry was making to end his message was that Billy Sunday was now 'with Christ.' The Bible is clear how it will end for the believer (II Corinthians 5:1–8). When time for me

> will be no more in this life, then I am promised an audience 'with' Christ. 'That where He is, there I will be also' (John 14:1–3). There is a departure date in all of our lives: whether a death date or rapture date (I Thessalonians 4:13–17). 'With Him' is the best promise Christ ever gave us. What stage are you in today? My first challenge is for those who are 'without' Christ; come 'in' today (II Corinthians 6"2)! My last challenge is for those 'in' Christ, but not 'for' Christ. When you are finally 'with' Him there, you will wish you had been 'for' Him here!

Afterwards, we had supper with Pastor Chacho, his wife, and two daughters in their small apartment attached to the back of the church. We had egg curry (I won't even explain it) with ample kinds of fruits and Coke (yes, the American stuff). Once again the freedom by which these poor folks give of what they have humbled me and my daughter. Marnie enjoyed the interaction with the ladies in the kitchen area, while the men and I sat in the living room area talking. Once again the time went by quickly as we had to head for Kangazha and the very long and difficult road home. We had been all day, and the Church had waited all day for just a few swift and fleeting moments of fellowship; no doubt our last until Heaven! (Postscript: It was not our last for as I edit this remembrance, I have just returned from India and part of my third trip was a revisit of the mountain churches of the IGBC. Once again the fellowship was sweet and the road was long and difficult, another story for another time!)

9

To Kangazha on Bald Tires

II Corinthians 5:7—For we walk by faith, not by sight.

THE DAY before Marnie and I headed off to our Sunday safari to visit the brethren in the eastern mountains of Kerala, Shibu had told me of the long day (a 16-hour day) ahead. He also told me on our way home we would be traveling through a protected forest where wild elephant sightings were common. Ever since my first trip to India and my amazing elephant safari to Thekkadi where I did get to see elephants in the wild, I dreamed of another such sighting for my daughter. That night I prayed that the Good Lord would permit such an elephant encounter on our way home. Little did I know at the same time my traveling companions were praying for just the opposite!

We left Thompramkudy around 6:00 PM. The sun would be setting within the hour as we slowly made our way back down the mountains we had accented that morning. By the time darkness fell, we had entered the Kaiauva Forest. It was there I confessed my prayer request of the night before. Instantly, I could sense a change in the attitude in the car. At first, Shibu ignored my conversation and questions about when we might see a wild elephant. Finally, he told me very bluntly that to see a wild elephant at this time of the night would be a very dangerous event; an encounter that nobody in the car wanted, except me!

It was then I discovered just how scared the average Indian is of wild elephants. My only experiences had been positive and thrilling. I have not as yet developed even a bit of fear of the massive creatures. Shibu told me that there were certain pastors in the association that wouldn't even travel the road we were on in the dark for fear of encountering a wild elephant. Nevertheless, the more he warned the more I persisted in my desire to see one or two on our drive through Kaiauva Forest. Because of my fascination with these huge creatures, I wasn't going to be detoured in my hope and wish to see another one in the wilderness setting of mountainous Kerala. It was then that Shibu decided to put the matter to rest.

Turning to his brother Shaju and our driver Binu, he said:

> "Well, if the pastor persists and he does get a chance to see a wild elephant up close and personal than I vote to throw him out of the car and press on."

Everybody began to laugh and I too saw the humor in the statement, but I also understood that despite the joke Shibu was also serious. Elephants kill hundreds of people every year in India, and as we in Maine have come to have a healthy respect for the moose at night, so too have the Indians come to respect the power of a wild elephant after dark, or anytime of the day. The damage a wild elephant can do to a car traveling in their territory at night is beyond imagination. We saw no elephants during our dark decent, so I didn't have to experience Jonah's fate (Jonah 1:15); besides, we had other worries to confront!

While we were waiting at Koch Kamaksi for our service at Thompramkudy, Shaju and Binu went missing. On our way back home through the Kaiauva Forest we found out that the 'boys' had gone to check on a small cumin plantation the mission owns not far from the Koch Church. However, on their way there they had a flat tire, but hadn't been able to find a tire shop to repair the flat. We were running over very difficult roads with a spare that was flat!

As we traveled towards the Kaiauva Dam, we stopped in a couple of small towns to see if anybody would repair the flat tire. At each stop Shaju would say, if we can't find a repairman we will have to travel home on 'faith'! During one of those stops, I got out to stretch my legs (I was in the middle seat with very little leg room, and the trip was beginning to get to me. I can say in nearly 2000 miles I have traveled in India those 60 miles back to Edyappara were the toughest for me!) and happened to notice the front tires of Shibu's car. I thought to myself, we must be traveling on 'faith' because we are not traveling on much rubber!

The front tires on Shibu's car reminded me of a set of tires I drove home from college on in the early 1970s. Not having much money, and always trying to get the last mile out of my tires, I traveled 1500 miles back from South Carolina to Maine. The Lord was good to me then as He was the night we traveled back from Thompramkudy. I will never forget as long as I live the look of my father's face when I drove onto the homestead. He hardly said, "Hello", when he began to bring attention to the tires on his old 1964 Chevy. I hadn't even noticed that the tread was gone and the steel belts were showing through the side and the front of the tires. Why they weren't flat I don't know, but they were still inflated. It was then my father threatened me within an inch of my life to never again get in a car with bald tires. I had kept that promise; that is until the night Marnie and I drove back to Kangazha through the Kaiauva Forest in India!

On our way we had to descend nearly 10,000 feet through a series of hairpin turns beyond description. During one section of the road we made twelve hairpin turns in a row; back and forth, back and forth, falling straight down with each turn. Some sections of the road were very rough, and all I could think was, will the tires hold? They did as we made it back safely, so once again 'faith' had gotten us home. The very next day I was quick to give Shibu money for two new front tires, and as I gave him the money I told him the story of my father and my trip home from Bob Jones University. There was a smile on Shibu's face the next time we got into his car and headed out of town. "Did you notice the tires?" he asked. I hadn't, but when I did I saw two brand new tires. Sometimes you have to travel by 'faith', but there is nothing wrong with traveling on 'Goodyear' either; just ask my Dad!

10

The Bible Still Stands

II Timothy 3:16—All Scripture is given by inspiration . . .

FOR THE first time in India, I had fallen into bed exhausted. Our 166 mile marathon into the eastern hills of Kerala had taken us 16 hours to finish. The last three and a half hours home were the most difficult. As was my custom to record my day in my journal before bed, I opted for a good night's sleep instead. By 5:30 AM the next morning I was up writing and it was 7:00 AM before I finished. By that time the sun was up and time for me to switch gears. I needed to prepare for another 'first' in my life: my first ministry as a Bible Conference speaker!

As is the custom of Kerala Baptist Bible College, the days leading up to graduation were filled with conferences and nightly evangelistic meetings. Over the next four days, besides the Bible conference in the morning, my daughter Marnie would conduct a ladies conference and I would conduct a men's conference; both in the afternoon. What made these meetings so unique is that they would be held in 100 degree plus heat, and mostly outdoors! I challenge you to find one person in the United States that would attend a single session of a Bible conference in similar conditions? The dedication of these people to the Word of God has inspired me each and every time I have ministered among them.

As was her custom, Julie (Shibu's wife) had breakfast waiting for Marnie and me as we emerged from our rooms about eight. Her famous English toast and American eggs were on the table along side a bowl of fruit I didn't recognize. On my first trip to Edyappara, I had exposed myself to a variety of fruits that I had never tasted before. Fruit like: goa, papia, mango, chucka, and guava; along with four kinds of banana, pineapple, watermelon, apples and oranges. That first morning of the Bible conference I was going to add a truly Biblical fruit to my list of Indian sweets: pomegranate!

Pomegranate was one of the first fruits brought back from Canaan to the children of Israel to show the fruitfulness of the land. (Numbers 13:23) The fruit is mentioned throughout the Old Testament, and its shape was used for many a decoration in the tabernacle and the temple. I learned that the fruit comes from a shrub that can grow upwards to twenty feet. The fruit is about the size of an orange when fully grown. The skin is as tough as leather, and inside are many small seeds. The fruit is actually the sweet, juicy pulp that covers the seeds. Both Marnie and I enjoyed this new taste of India, and after a filling breakfast we were off to prepare for the speaking engagements of the day.

Marnie had chosen to speak on certain topics of the Bible and what they teach the women of Kerala of God's hand on their lives. I had determined to share with the men some of my favorite Biblical heroes and what their lives could teach us. For the Bible Conference itself, my title was taken from an old church hymn: 'The Bible Stands.' My twist in that theme was 'The Bible Still Stands' and my key verse was Psalms 100:5: "For the Lord is good; His mercy is everlasting; and His truth endureth to all generations."

My opening message at the KBBC Bible Conference that Monday morning was based on these words from Haldor Lillenas' chorus: "The Bible stands though the hills may tumble, it will firmly stand when the earth shall crumble; I will plant my feet on its firm foundation, for the Bible stands." I went on to share these three reasons why I believe the Bible still stands today in India and around the world:

1. Why, Because It Is Still Inspired. II Timothy 3:15–17. All teachings about the Bible must start, in my opinion, with this belief. I believe what the Bible says about itself: A) It is 'holy' Scripture (II Timothy 3:15). The word 'holy' means 'being set apart.' As God is set apart unto holiness, so is the Word of God. The Bible is a book set apart from all other books. B) It is 'all' Scripture (II Timothy 3:16). Without exception; "All" of it; all the way from Genesis to Malachi and beyond, I feel that Matthew to Revelation can be included in this word 'all'! All books, all chapters, all verses, all words, all stories are included as well. Once you remove one letter into the category of 'unbelief', then the rest falls. C) It is 'inspired' Scripture (II Timothy 3:16). The word 'inspired' means 'God-breathed.' We are not saying just the thoughts are of God, but the very words are from God (Thus Saith The Lord). Human in penmanship, but Divine in authorship!

2. Why, Because It Is Inerrant. Titus 1:2. Inspired therefore inerrant. We have concluded that they are God's words not Moses' words, or Isaiah's words. If they are God's words then they are honest and true and without error; therefore trustworthy. They can be totally, absolutely believed because they come from a God that cannot lie. The omniscient God, the all-knowing God which includes foreknowledge, forth knowledge, and full-knowledge (Psalms 139:1–6) makes the Scriptures authentic and authoritative whether your speaking about Geology (Genesis 1:1), History (Daniel 5), Archeology (Joshua 2:1), Geography (Luke 19:28), Biology (I Corinthians 15:39), Prophecy (II Peter 1:20–21), Anthropology (Genesis 1:27), or Astronomy (I Corinthians 15:41).

3. Why, Because It Is Infallible. Matthew 5:18. Distinctly, decisively, definitely the Word of God contains God's Truth; without falsehood or error. It will stand the test of time and critics, for it is pointedly, precisely, and powerfully the Word of God (Hebrews 4:12), and we can use it to tell others of the thoughts and intents of the mind of God (Titus 2:1,7,8). I believe this precept in the Proverbs of Solomon says it best: "Every word of God is pure: He is a shield unto them that put their trust in Him." (Proverbs 30:5) What is true of Him is true of His word! "I stand alone on the Word of God", for you cannot only sing it, you can believe it as well!

11

Half a Million Rupees for Venmony

II Corinthians 8:14—But by equality, that now at this time your abundance may be a supply for their want . . .

YOU CAN'T walk the roadways of Edyappara without knowing you are treading in a heathen, Hindu land.

One of the first shocks in Kerala in 2006 was numerous sightings of the Nazi swastika symbol. I will never forget my first reaction as I walked from the orphanage to Annamma's house. There in the grate work of a neighbor's house was the evil symbol of Nazism. I was dumb founded. All that came to my mind was the terrible exploits of Nazi Germany during World War II. I was especially offended because that era in history has been of particular interest to me since the seventh grade. I have literally read hundreds of books on the Second World War, and throughout those books have been that ensign. That image had only one meaning to me, and I was stunned to find it in the peaceful village of Edyappara, India.

I immediately asked Shibu why such a hated symbol could be found in his village. He didn't know, and didn't seem to be as shocked as I was to find it just down the street.

Over my next 40-days in his state, I saw the symbol everywhere, but couldn't discover its meaning. When I pointed out the swastika to my daughter on my second trip to Kerala, she too was surprised to see it displayed in the open. In most of the world this ensign is deplored, and if exposed, destroyed, and yet in the State of Kerala it seemed to be a very open and accepted symbol, but for what? Surely, there was a logical explanation for the area wide use of such an appalling emblem?

Interestingly, it wasn't until I returned to Maine that I discovered the logical answer to my question of the swastika. I had just picked up my son from the Greyhound Bus Station in Bangor when he asked me to drive him over to a local car dealership to look at a car. Scott is in the United States Army. He is stationed at Fort Bragg, North Carolina, and he was home for a ten-day furlough. Scott was looking to buy a car so he wouldn't have to take the 26-hour bus ride back to base. As he talked with the salesman, I read a Time magazine. To my surprise, in the third "Time" I leafed through there was the answer to my most puzzling question from India. Under the caption of "Confusing Signs" I read this:

> Hindus are protesting Germany's move to forbid the swastika in the European Union-a ban that already exists in some countries because of the symbol's link to Nazism, right? But the crooked cross has also been a Hindu sign of peace for 5000 years. Symbols often have multiple sides!

How narrow-minded I felt! Such is the teaching of Romans 12:18: "If it be possible, as much as lieth in you live peaceably with all men (including Hindus)." My brothers and sisters in Edyappara had taught me another valuable lesson in dealing with the strange culture that is Kerala. It is often good to learn why before you assume something evil, and now I understood why I had come to India a second time. Oh, I had come to be the graduation speaker for the KBBC class of 2007, but I was also on a mission from my Church in Ellsworth to bring a gift of peace to the saints in Venmony and their Hindu neighbors.

One of the burdens I returned from India with in 2006 was for a small flock of saints in Venmony, Kerala. The work had been established in the mid-1980s, but for over twenty years the believers had been homeless. Every other church plant in Kerala had been able to establish a house of worship, but not Venmony. It had taken them all these years just to scrap together enough money to buy a piece of land, but to build a sanctuary was still decades off!

My one trip to Venmony on a Sunday evening in 2006 had convinced me that I should do something to help. The motivation behind the desire was simple. The young pastor Regi Matthews and his young family (wife Sinue and daughter Abiya) reminded me of my church plant in 1973, and how my wife and I and a young son struggled to establish a church in Pembroke, New Hampshire. We had to move four times in five years, and never were able to find or build a permanent worship place. As I returned to Maine, a vision began to form in my heart.

Returning to the Emmanuel Baptist Church in Ellsworth, Maine, I began to challenge its members with the possibility of us building the folks at Venmony a sanctuary, but with a twist. I had also discovered in my first trip to Kerala that none of the other 18 churches of the IGBC had parsonages, a very difficult handicap for the pastors. Most of the pastors have to travel many miles from their homes to pastor their churches. Why not add a parsonage to the plans for Venmony? I had talked to Shibu about my vision before I left, and he had an engineer draw up the plans and the basic cost. I laid it all out to the people of Emmanuel Baptist Church, and the rest is, as they say, history.

On February 24, 2007, Marnie and I traveled to Venmony with the Simon family to present to the people of the Venmony Baptist Church a check for $12,279. Not a member of the church, or the pastor knew that we were coming for that reason. They thought we were just coming for a revisit. Even Shibu and Shaju didn't know that we had raised the entire amount in just under a year. They thought we had come simply to give a down payment for the project. Marnie had come up with the idea of a church portrait of the people of Emmanuel to also give so that the people of Venmony might know who had given them this great gift. Needless to say, the tears flowed as the plans were present, then the check (in rupees 537,206.25), and finally the plague with the church people's picture on it!

A few years ago Emmanuel thought about building on the side of its existing sanctuary a gym and kitchen. Those plans fell through because God wanted them instead to build a church in India for some very precious brethren there. The structure will contain no swastikas, but it will stand as a testimony to the Prince of Peace in a very hostile place.

Postscript: It took over three years to build the church sanctuary and parsonage because of the resistance of the Hindu authorities in the town. I, eventually, had the privilege along with a deacon, Russ Coffin, of the Emmanuel Baptist Church to travel to Venmony and to dedicate the building on February 28, 2010.

12

Messages in Malayalam

Ezekiel 3:6— . . . too many people of a strange speech and of a hard language, whose words thou canst not understand . . .

OF THE 35 messages Marine and I were able to deliver in India on our 12-day stay in Kerala, 31 of them were spoken in Malayalam (interestingly, spelled the same both frontward and backward).

Marnie had experienced the joy of speaking through a translator on her previous short-term mission trips to Africa. I had also come to enjoy the pleasure of preaching through an interpreter on my trip to Edyappara the year before. That freedom of thought and presentation came back very quickly to both Marnie and me as we shared the messages the Good Lord had laid on our hearts for this trip.

In Puthur, Marnie spoke on the 'faithfulness of God' according to Psalms 139:7–10; at Kangazha on the 'goodness of God' according to I Thessalonians 5:24; at 504 Colony that 'God can save even a child' according to the story of Jarius' daughter; at Venmony on the 'provision of God' according to Mark 5; at Koch Kamakshi on how 'God can be seen' according to Hebrews 12:2, and at Thompramkudy on how 'God can fulfill dreams' according to I Peter 2:25. Either Shaju or Shibu translated for Marnie at these church services. For her three-day ladies conference, Marnie used Psalms 139:15–18 to teach how God can use us; the woman at the well in John 4 to teach God's saving grace, and finally Ephesians 1:3 to speak of the wonderful spiritual blessings that are ours in Christ. Reneeshya Ariachacil, the college librarian, was Marnie's interpreter for this series of meetings. Marnie also taught two lessons to the kids at the orphanage: Jesus' feeding the 5000 and Jonah and the fish. Shibu acted as Marnie's translator on both those occasions. Marnie's last message in Malayalam took place during the farewell service at the Kangazha Church when she spoke on "My India Blessings." A difficult language made easy by those who have the ability to translate one tongue into another!

I on the other hand am a preacher who likes 'series.' For this India trip I had brought along two that I hoped to share in one fashion or another. For my men's conference I would speak on Shamgar: The Unknown Hero (Judges 3:31); Jabez: The Unnoticed Hero (I Chronicles 4:9–10), and Caleb: The Unsung Hero (Numbers 13:6). For the Bible Conference I adapted a series I call: 'They Call Me Old Fashion.' In that series I spoke on 'old fashion' scriptures, standards, service, and the second coming of Christ. The rest of my messages were 'general' sermons I had brought along to share as the Holy Spirit led me. I too was teamed up with some of my translators from my first visit to India in 2006, as well as some new interpreters, like Joshi Abraham and Bobby Kuriakose. As before, these men made ministry easy. To me, this is the purest form of preaching there is, for one must rely on the Holy Spirit's leading to get the message across, like the first message I preached at the nightly evangelistic service during Bible conference week at Kerala Baptist Bible College. The title of my sermon that night was "Whatever Happened to Hell?"

Did you know that Jesus spoke of hell 56 times in His sermons, yet He only spoke of Heaven 24 times? In Jesus very first recorded sermon, The Sermon On The Mount, (Matthew 5–7) He spoke about Hell. In Jesus last recorded sermon, The Olivet Discourse, (Matthew 24) He also spoke about Hell. Jesus would be labeled today, a hell-fire and brimstone preacher! So why has the word suddenly been taken out of the vocabulary of most preachers today? It has become the favorite swear word of the ungodly, but the Church has lost interest in warning of this terrible place. The Bible certainly doesn't ignore the subject, why do we? There are revisionists that would have us remove it all together from our pulpits, so whatever happened to hell? So what has changed?

1. *A Changed Purpose.* Matthew 25:41. Jesus tells us that the original purpose for hell was for 'the devil and his angels.' Today, only child-molesters, serial killers, and terrorists are going to burn in hell? Interestingly, no mention of hell in Genesis 1:1; then came along Isaiah 14: Satan's fall from grace. So a place for him was found, and all those that fell with him. Good people, righteous people, moral people have decided that they are not like the devil, so no hell for them. The tragic result of such a philosophy is a whole lot of people are going to hell and they don't even know it. Human sin, individual sin has changed the purpose of hell.

2. *A Change of Perimeter*. Isaiah 5:14. I believe hell is actually growing, getting bigger, and constantly expanding. There are some scientists that say they have discovered an expanding universe. Is it possible for places to expand? Isaiah says, "Enlarged herself" about hell! Why is it getting bigger? (Matthew 7:13) Just the angels alone, a (Revelation 12:4) third of a number 'without measure' would cause it to grow. The teaching seems clear to me; a place that can never get full (Proverbs 27:20) because it is ever expanding. Think about that? Of a population that once numbered probably as many as are on the planet now just before the Flood, and only 8 survived, and the rest went to hell; this is a big place, and the sad truth that it is growing because the number of people going there is growing!
3. *A Change of People?* Isaiah 14:9. Note if you will, the question mark on this point. Surely when people get to hell they will change? Is revival possible in hell? Can one repent in hell? Read carefully Luke 16:23–31 and the only change you see in hell from the rich man was his concern about his brothers not going there. (Revelation 22:11 and 21:8) You will take your nature to hell, and you will not change. Cain will still be wandering; Ahab will still be looking for a vineyard to steal, and Achan will still be hiding his loot! Hell: a prepared place for a perverted people, with a perimeter ever pushing outward, and permanent!

As I warned the residents of Edyappara, I warn those who read this. Hell is a real place, and if you don't want to go there then it is vital that you receive Jesus Christ as your Saviour (Acts 16:30). Believe in what He did for you on Calvary and you will immediately change paths (Matthew 7:13–14). Believe and receive and Heaven will be your new destination (Romans 10:9–13)!

13

Auto Ride around Edyappara

Jeremiah 51:41— . . . and how is the praise of the whole earth surprised . . .

PRINTED IN the front of my second India journal is this verse:

> And some days after Paul said unto Barnabas, Let us go again and visit our brethren in every city where we have preached the Word of the Lord, and see how they do. (Acts 15:36)

Almost from the day I got back from India the first time, this verse was on my heart. I knew that I wouldn't be able to revisit all the places I traveled to and all the people I had preached to on my first trip (12 churches), but I could revisit the special places and people of my home away from home: Edyappara. Besides, I wanted my daughter to know why this village in Kerala had become so very special to me. Also on my 'to-do' list for my second trip to India was something that I failed to do on my first time there: take an auto (the famous three-wheeled carts of India) ride. I am glad now that I waited because my first 'auto-ride' was with Marnie.

Jacob John is a member of the Kangazha Church, the key board player for the Heavenly Singers (the singing group of the mission), and an 'auto' driver by profession. I made arrangements for him to meet Marnie and I for a morning run around Edyappara. At eight o'clock sharp John was in front of the new residential building of the college. His traditional yellow and black auto was no stranger to the back lanes and side roads of his home town. After a few pictures, both outside and inside his auto, we headed out of town to see the mission's rubber tree plantation, and then Big Stream. Because of walking restrictions to these places, I knew this would be the best way for Marnie to see the places I had talked so much about after my first trip.

The putt-putt-putt of the auto echoed off the numerous rock walls we passed along the way. The rubber trees flashed by as we quickly made our way from here to there. On every hill Jacob John shut his auto off and coasted down hill to save gas! The wind felt refreshing in our faces as the early morning temperature passed 95 heading for another 100 plus day. The trees at the plantation had been put to bed (as they say), for the dry season that was coming, so Marnie couldn't witness the traditional way they make rubber. Big Stream, where we had the annual baptism the year before, was barely flowing. The stream was nothing more than a series of small muddy ponds in the creek bed. Still the joy of seeing the place again brought back great memories; it was still my Jordan River; that is until I visit the original one! (A trip I will take with my daughter in May of 2010 with a group from Dallas Theological Seminary.)

After visiting these two very special places, we traveled across town to Sarah's house. I had met this blind lady one afternoon while on visitation with Shibu. The 'boys' former children's church teacher, Sarah reminded me of my mother-in-Christ, the lady who had lead me to Jesus, Lily Harris: my children's church teacher. I wanted Marnie to meet Sarah, but more importantly I wanted Sarah to meet Marnie. (It would be our last visit this side of heaven because shortly after Marnie and I got back to the States Sarah made the journey to her heavenly home. I can't wait for our next visit!) What a joy it is to revisit the brethren, even if it is only for a few fleeting minutes.

Each and every time I ventured out into the village of Edyappara, I usually was surprised by something: something new, something unexpected, something fascinating, something unusual, something worthy of praise. Marine's auto ride around the town to visit old friends and memorable places also produced one of these unexpected surprises.

We had stopped by the local cemetery to show Marnie how they bury people in India, when from across the road a lady carrying a container of water on her head was recognized by my daughter. Marnie is very gifted in cross-cultural relationships. Her out-going personality and people skills allow her to instantly blend into any environment: Edyappara only verified this ability to me. Within moments Marnie was across the street and carrying on a conversation with this lady from the Kangazha Church, a lady Marnie had meet in our first service. For me, I still see 'brown' most of the time; most Indians look alike to me, yet Marnie has that ability to see faces, not color.

Marnie also has been given a great ability in language. I was in India 40-days and picked up just a few words. We had only been in India five-days and already Marnie was able to understand some Malayalam. Soon a group of people were gathered around my daughter, including our faithful driver Binu (whose real name is Roshan Joseph). Binu's parent's house was just across from the cemetery. Marnie was showing the gathering the pictures she had taken on our auto ride around town (the miracle of a digital camera). After a few minutes of fellowship, we were off again with Jacob John.

After a short trip up through the hills and hollows of north Edyappara, we were returning to the college passing the cemetery again when there by the road was Binu. He had changed his cloths, and waved us down to ask if we might come to his home to meet his parents. We drove into the typical front yard of the average Kangazha home. They had a few goats, a few chickens, and a cow walking around. They tapped a few rubber trees for income, and their hospitality was India like: exceptional. We were greeted like a king and a princess. Little did I know that one of Marnie's desires on this trip was to drink coconut milk straight from the shell, and to eat fresh coconut? It wasn't long before Binu's dad was cutting down a coconut from one of his coconut trees. Within minutes, Jacob John had cut off the top of the coconut and Marnie had her first taste (she really liked it).

It wasn't long after that first drink that Binu had broken the coconut open and was cutting thin strips of fresh coconut with his knife. Marnie and I both enjoyed the sweet, soft taste of freshly cut coconut, an unexpected treat on our auto ride around Edyappara to visit old friends and to make new ones.

14

An Orphan Is Adopted

Galatians 4:5—To redeem them that were under the law, that they might receive the adoption of sons.

THE LAST night of the evangelistic crusade in Edyappara turned out to be a very special night. Here is the outline of the message I simply called "Mercy and Grace":

Rare are the places in the Bible were mercy and grace are side by side, or is it so rare? Before I visited India for the second time, I finished reading David Jeremiah's book, "Captured by Grace." I was challenged to look a bit closer to the similar stories of the Bible, to see if mercy and grace could be found in them. Let me illustrate what I found in three very familiar stories from God's word, and the application David Jeremiah taught me:

1. *Mercy Withheld the Knife; and Grace Provided the Lamb*. Genesis 22:12–13. This is perhaps the most dramatic story in the life of Abraham; I know it is the most amazing story in the life of Isaac. For the first time I have seen this test of Abraham's faith in the light of the test of Job's faith. Like with Job, for years God had put a hedge (Job 1:10) around Isaac; that is

until that early morning wakeup call by God. What the Devil never learns in such trials is that 'mercy and grace' always linger near by. Just when Satan thought he had killed 'the son of promise' by Abraham's own hand mercy stepped in, and just a few steps behind came grace, a perfect picture in my opinion of the wonders of Calvary. The substitution was made by grace because mercy had been alert to the danger near God's man!

2. *Mercy Runs to the Prodigal and Grace Puts on a Meal.* Luke 15:20–23. One of Christ's great stories also contains the precept we are underlining and highlighting in this message. How often I have read this story and even preached on this parable, but failed to see mercy and grace at work. They are not mentioned in the story, as with the story of Abraham and Isaac, but they are found in the message. I can honestly say the older brother had neither, but the father had both. Undeserved, unwarranted, unexpected, but is not that what mercy and grace are all about? Mercy and grace always show up where the 'Father' can be found (II Corinthians 1:2–3). This is why you will only find this 'brand of love' in the Father's house?
3. *Mercy Bound the Wounds, and Grace Paid All the Bills*. Luke 10:34–35. Once again in one of Christ's classic parables we see this combination again at work. The ones (priest and Levite) who should have shown mercy and grace were found with none. The one (Samaritan) we would expect to have neither showed both. Would it not have been enough to help

> the man caught by robbers, but to pay his expenses as well, 'going above and beyond the call of mercy'? Mercy is never just enough with God. For many it is, but Jesus came to teach us a different way of looking at life and the lives of those we are called on to help. Jesus taught us to go the 'extra mile' (Matthew 5:41); mercy is the mile, and grace is the extra mile!

Now let me tell you 'the rest of the story'!

The last evangelistic service during the annual Bible conference at KBBC for 2007 took place on a Wednesday night. Each night we saw crowds of well over 250 gathering in the courtyard of the college. As with any India service, there was plenty of singing, specials, and supplication. I was especially blessed by a quartet (three boys and a girl), all from Assam (a state in northeastern India), who sang a Southern Gospel song. (Talk about getting out of your comfort zone?) They were very good and Marnie and I enjoyed a taste of home on that hot and steamy evening.

I had been fighting an Indian cold (how was that possible in such heat?) all week, and a painful mouth canker since our arrival in Edyappara. Despite the physical shortcomings, I had learned through similar situations in the past to keep on preaching (II Timothy 4:2), for at such times the Lord works His wonderful mercy and grace. Paul was right when he wrote, "Therefore I take pleasure in infirmities . . . for when I am weak, then am I strong." (II Corinthians 12:10)

I spoke over a half an hour (over an hour with translation) on the theme of mercy and grace. The heart of the message was simple: that wherever the mercy of God abides, grace is not far behind. As I finished my three Biblical illustrations on this concept, I sat down exhausted, blowing my nose because of my head cold, and drinking water with considerable pain from my canker. The Gospel preacher was weak, but the Gospel was strong.

Shibu gave the invitation, and when he asked for 'hands' from the crowd only one thin, brown hand rose from the front row. It was the hand of Subin Samuel, one of the orphans from the Mercy Home (the name of the orphanage of the Simon ministry). God has such an amazing sense of poetic justice. As I watched Shibu lead Subin to the Lord after the last hymn, I decided I would give my evening message a new title: from 'Mercy and Grace' to "An Orphan Is Adopted"! Paul proclaimed the doctrine of 'adoption', but few are preaching it today. Yet for an orphan boy in India, it might just be the greatest truth that can be proclaimed. Subin Samuel now is "a son of God" (John 1:12), 'heir of God' and a joint-heir with Christ (Romans 8:14–17), and now part of 'the family of God' (Ephesians 3:15)!

After Shibu told me the story of Subin, for he would be our only visible conversion of the trip, I thought again of Jesus' teaching in His parable of the lost silver: "Likewise, I say unto you, there is joy in the presence of the angels of God over one sinner that repenteth;" (Luke 15:10) as there was in Edyappara, India that memorable Indian night.

15

School Bus Ride around Kangazha

Proverbs 4:1—Hear, ye children,
the instruction of a father and attend
to know understanding.

ANOTHER ONE of the places I had to take Marnie during my second trip to Edyappara was Bethany Christian English Medium School, Annamma Simon's ministry. This was not only a mission ministry, but the school of my new little friend, Joshua Sackson, or as I called him 'little sipe', or little white man.

Joshua and I had become great friends during my time with him and his family the previous winter. We had many grand adventures together, and he was the first to call me 'big sipe.' Joshua had been born in the United States while his Dad was going to Bible School (Dallas Theological Seminary, interestingly where Marnie is studying for her Masters). In some respects, though he looks like any Indian lad, Jos is more American than Indian. He was having a hard time adjusting when I was with him the first time, and I found during my second visit few changes in the culture and customs of his native land. His Malayalam was much better, but he still craved American food and American ways; he was still 'little sipe' to me!

While I was with Jos the first time, he had started school. Despite the fact the school is based upon the English language (a highly desired skill in India), the school is still very Indian in nature. The typical English style of uniform is required. The sever discipline is there. Joshua was doing very well when Marnie and I arrived for our visit. He was the top student in his class; yet you could tell by his ways that he still felt out of place, a stranger in his own land. It was for this reason I asked my little friend if Marnie and I might attend his class and meet his classmates. I wanted to be an encouragement to him, and also let Marnie experience a typical Indian school and the 'hollywood' atmosphere that happens when a white person comes to an Indian private school.

The minute Marnie raised Karen's camera to take her first picture it began. Streaming out of the building came scores of brown faced boys and girls. They flocked around Marnie like she was the Pied Piper of Hamelin. I watched as the ancient German legend unfolded before my eyes. Wherever Marnie went with her flute (camera) there was a group of children following her. Browning's poem played itself out in the courtyard of the Bethany School and its classrooms!

The first question of the kids was 'What is your name?' They had remembered me, but had forgotten my name. Once I introduced them to Marnie and retold them my name all we heard as we walked around was 'Marnie, Barry; Marnie, Barry; Marnie, Barry!' As was their custom, we had to sign a number of autograph books. I have never gone to the Bethany School without coming back feeling like a celebrity. Even in Joshua's classroom and around Joshua's classmates, we were cheered and touched and questioned as famous visitors. Joshua was also seen in a different light because of his American friends. My prayer is that my little white man's adjustment will come quickly; without to much more difficulty.

Another one of the great memories of my first trip to India was a school bus ride around town with a bus driver called Bijew. He is just one of three drivers that pick up the kids for the Bethany School. I also wanted my daughter to experience that side of Kerala school life, so on the morning of March 1, 2007 Marnie and I made the early run just before the last session of the Bible Conference.

Marnie is by her very nature an amazing ambassador. She has always had the ability to be polite and friendly to whoever she meets. On that school bus ride to pick up some of the kids and a few of the staff of Bethany, I saw this 'gift' exhibited to each brown-face child that boarded the small, light brown school bus. Setting up front with Bijew, Marnie greeted the students and staff with a friendly namastay ('good morning'). Because the Bethany School is an English-speaking only school, the language barrier that resists most attempts to communicate was not a problem that morning on Bijew's bus. The kids were shy at first, and some looked away as they did on my first bus ride around Edyappara and beyond, but it wasn't long before Marnie had everyone smiling back and saying in their heavy Indian accent, 'good morning'!

In our 50-minute bus ride, we traveled to Partathanam before eventually working our way back to Edyappara by way of Big Stream. My bus ride the year before had taken us along another route, so it was nice for me to make a few more connections and help me understand more clearly the road system that is Kangazha. A few more questions on 'where does that road lead' were answered on this trip. On the way (Bijew's first run, all three drivers have two routes to pick up the nearly 300 students) we would pick up 25 students and 2 teachers and one special delivery and a few transfer passengers.

Two events on this run seemed strange to me. First, it wasn't long before we started to pick up passengers that were too old to be students at Bethany. They might ride for a few miles then Bijew would stop and they would get off. One elderly lady in particular drew my attention; it was then I realized that Bijew was also carting around town old people that had to walk a long distance to a local bus stop, or there was no bus near their home so they caught a ride with Bijew. Second, halfway through the trip Bijew stopped and a lady by the road handed a package to the attendant that helped the kids on the bus. We were nearly back to the school when, without even stopping, that same package was handed off to another man standing beside the road. Bijew was also the UPS man of Kangazha.

After a few great pictures Marnie and I let the kids go to their classrooms, and with a final wave and 'have a nice day', we walked back to our room having been taught another great 'lesson from India'!

16

Of Friendships and Fellowship

Proverbs 14:20— . . . But the rich hath many friends.

I HAVE always considered myself to be a rich man when it came to friends, but my wealth increased dramatically when I went to India in the winter of 2006.

One of the reasons for my desire to return to India with my daughter was to revisit and introduce Marnie to some of my newest friends. Little did I realize the impact my Indian friends would have on my daughter, especially, the friendship I had developed with a young man who was just old enough to be my son.

Following my meeting with the men (more later) and Marnie's meeting with the women at KBBC, we headed across town to visit the Joy Thomas family. Despite the shortness of time, he was one of the individuals I wanted to spend sometime with. Joy and I had become close friends during my first visit. We had traveled many miles together visiting churches, and as he would tell you; he came along to be my 'bodyguard.' Despite the fact he barely stands five feet tall, and I am six foot, the title of 'bodyguard' remains. Joy Thomas is the director of the missionary outreach of the IGBC churches in the State of Orissa. Joy is from Kerala, but has a missionary heart for the unreached. His work in that northern state has earned him the title of 'the Paul of Orissa.' Over the years he has started twenty churches, and the work continues to grow despite great persecution. (2008 would see some of the worst persecution in the states history with many giving their lives for the cause of Christ.) He can't actually live in Orissa because of the threats on his life.

Our fellowship was sweet as we visited with his wife and three children, but I could see that my daughter was getting anxious to move on. Marnie had an invitation from Binu to go on a motorcycle ride to the river. The afternoon was quickly passing, and with it the light. If she was to go with Binu, we had to say goodbye to the Thomas family. We took a last picture, picked up our orange soda (a gift), and we headed back across town to the college. Our timing was perfect, for as we reached the second floor of the residential building the cry was heard from Abigail (the Simon's little girl), "Ana, Ana, Ana"! (Elephant) Sure enough a working, forest elephant was lumbering down the lane that separated the building we were living in from the college campus. This was Marnie's first up close and personal look at India's massive creature; a bird's eye view no less. We snapped plenty of pictures as the elephant made its way down the street and out of sight to the woods beyond.

Shortly after the elephant disappeared, Binu arrived on the mission's motorcycle. Off the two new friends went to explore more of the surrounding area. After Marnie returned she shared with me the adventure she had as she rode to the local river and back. On the way they sighted the elephant again on the other side of Mundathanam. One of the pleasures of this trip to India this year was watching the growth of a friendship between an Indian lad and an American lass!

Another friend I was anxious to see and to introduce Marnie too was Jaldev Andhkury. Jaldev had been one of my students the year before, a graduate of the class of 2006. Jaldev had decided to come back for a Master's program that KBBC had just started, and it had been and was my privilege to pay for Jaldev to finish that course of study. (Name me a university or college where a young man can get a two years Master's Degree for only $600, and that includes room and board and all tuition!)

I don't know why Jaldev and I have hit it off, but almost from the first day as his American professor (what he calls me) I have been drawn to this 24-year old young man from Chhatisgarh State in north central India. Maybe, it is his infectious smile, his easy manner, or his polite nature. His is by Indian standards of an average height and build, and his character reflects the culture and custom he was raised in, but so where the other students of KBBC. Yet Jaldev and I have become deep friends, perhaps, because of the reoccurring interest he has always had for my family?

Despite the year of separation, Jaldev and I had kept in touch through letters, cards, and e-mails. Before I left India for the first time, Jaldev gave me a letter for my wife, and he did the same thing when Marnie and I left the second time. To show the nature of this dear lad, I share with you that letter:

Dear Auntie: Greetings to you in the name of our Lord and Savior Jesus Christ from India. This is my great joy and privilege to wire you once again. I do hope that this teller will find you well. I would like to thank you for allowing my beloved professor and spiritual father, and sister Marnie to make this trip to India. I was blessed and challenged by the presence and teachings, preaching and Bible classes of my professor and testimony of sister Marnie. Also this is my desire that would you please come to India maybe by next trip. I heard that brother Scott is getting training in U.S. Army which seems dangerous. I am praying for his protection. Continually, I ask your valuable prayers for my summer ministry, if God willing, I will be joining my father this summer. I am too, praying, for your health and ministry! Thanking you. You're Son in Christ. Jaldev K. Andhkury India.

After the second night's evangelistic meeting, Jaldev and I got to talk (he has better than average English skills) about his home state and the great need there. He gave me a formal invitation to come, and if I did he would be my translator. For me it was, like Paul, when he heard the man of Macedonia's invitation. God willing, I will make that journey someday to visit my new young friend in his hometown and ministry with him and his father in the mission field that is Bastar!

17

They Call Me Old-Fashion

John 15:10—If ye keep my commandments; ye shall abide in my love; even as I have kept my Father's commandments, and abide in His love.

I had two ministries during the days leading up to graduation (in the evening I preached at an evangelistic service conducted at the school): a morning challenge to the student body and staff and an afternoon class for visiting pastors and male students at the school (Marnie had a class for the pastor's wives and women at the college). My morning theme was 'The Bible Stands' and one message in that series was based on Mrs. C. D. Martin's classic church hymn:

"They call me old-fashion because I believe that the Bible is God's Holy Word. . . . I am bound to do right. . . . My sin was old-fashion, my guilt was old-fashion, God's love was old-fashion, I know; and the way I was saved was the old-fashion way, through the blood that makes whiter than snow!"

In this message I preached on the importance of establishing sound Biblical standards. Here is the outline to that message:

1. *Never Establish a Standard that Will Give Provision to the Flesh.* Romans 13:14. Read carefully Galatians 5:13. Old-fashion standards never make provision for the flesh to fulfill the lust of the flesh. God's Word knew of the nature of man after the fall, and there are no standards in the Book that will allow the flesh to continue on with sin.
2. *Never Establish a Standard that Could Produce and Evil Habit.* I Corinthians 6:12. Nobody takes a drink with the intent of becoming a drunk. Nobody takes drugs with the intent of becoming an addict. Read carefully I Corinthians 3:16–17. We are to see our bodies as the property of God and a residence of the Holy Spirit, and not an instrument to be used or abused as we will. There are good habits we should seek, but to establish a pattern by which we are hooked on a habit that eventually will control us is not a godly standard!
3. *Never Establish a Standard that You Can't Publish Openly and Freely.* I Peter 2:16. Do you hide, cover up, and lie about your standards? Can you share with all just what you believe about certain things? If you have to hide your standards from anyone; then you ought to consider carefully just how important those standards are. Read Galatians 5:22–23; these are the standards of God in which no law has been created against them. You ought to judge your standards by such standards. (Proverbs 6:16–19: the other side of this issue!)

4. *Never Establish a Standard that Will Be a Problem to Other.* I Corinthians 8:9. As believers our first consideration is not ourselves, but others. How will our standards affect others? (I Corinthians 8:13) I was taught from a very early age to consider all my actions in light of my parents and grandparents. What I did, how would it affect my mother and my father? Could I do what I was going to do, and would what I did bring honor to my grandfather and grandmother? Proper standards will not offend or hurt those we love.

Now it is your turn to go to your list of standards and see where they stack up to these simple precepts from God's Word. What will you find? It is so very important that we base our standards on the time-tested guidelines that have served the people of God well throughout the centuries!

That afternoon I shared this outline with the men on one of the unsung heroes of the Old Testament based on this Scripture:

> And Jabez was more honorable than his brethren: and his mother called his name Jabez, saying, because I bare him with sorrow. And Jabez called on the God of Israel, saying, Oh that Thou wouldest bless me indeed, and enlarge my coast, and that Thine hand might be with me, and that Thou wouldest keep me from evil, that it may not grieve me. And God granted him that which he requested. (I Chronicles 4:9–10)

The last place anybody wants to read during a reading-through-the Bible-in-a-year calendar is I Chronicles 1–12. How often have we bypassed those chapters thinking: just a bunch of names! I decided I would do my best to see why God put those dozen chapters in His inspired Word: what a blessing! Interestingly, about the same time I found this portion of God's Word, so did the world with the instant fame of "The Prayer of Jabez" book. I would like to share what I discovered in that now famous supplication:

1. *Jabez Prayed to Be Productive.* "Bless me, enlarge my coast." No doubt Jabez was a farmer, or a shepherd and he was asking for a bigger farm, a bigger flock. I too am the son of a farmer, a dairyman and I know what more land and more lambs involve: more work! This is not a strange request even in the spiritual sense. Read carefully John 15:1–16 in Jesus' classic message on "The Vine and the Branches." Trace the 'more' and 'much' of that message and you will see that the Husbandman asks for the same thing as Jabez! Paul asks for it in Romans 1:13, but have you?
2. *Jabez Prayed to Be Powerful.* "That Thine hand might be with me." This is a logical second petition because without the mighty hand of God being with him it would be impossible to take care of the first request. Without God's help we can't increase our work for Him (II Timothy 1:7) Have you ever asked the question, "How can I do more?" You can't, but He can, and as Paul learned: "I can do all things through Christ which strengtheneth me!" (Philippians 4:13) God wants us to ask of Him something so big that when it happens we know it was of God! Isn't that what happened to Gideon? William Carey, the famous

missionary to India, once said, "Ask great things of God, except great things of God!"

3. *Jabez Prayed to Be Protected.* "Keep me from evil." Jabez knew that if he was productive and powerful that he, like Job, would catch the eye of the 'wicked one.' There is this misconception that it is only the weak and wicked Christian that the Devil is after. He has already tripped them up, for it is the 'righteous' and the 'good' that he is after (I Corinthians 10:13). Paul was watchful (I Corinthians 9:27) and so was Jesus (Matthew 6:13), and so should we!

We could go a long way to find a better example of a godly prayer than 'the prayer of Jabez', and to think we would have missed it because the first twelve chapters of First Chronicles is just a list of name!

18

Wal-Mart Comes to Kottayam

Deuteronomy 28:8—The Lord shall command the blessing upon thee in thy storehouses . . .

On Thursday morning I preached my final message at the KBBC Bible Conference. Now it was time for Marnie and me to accomplish a few more desires on our India 'to-do' list.

My wife Coleen couldn't come with us on this trip to India, but she had nevertheless given us some instructions on what she wanted Marnie and me to do for her while in Kerala. Coleen had been burdened for the orphans of the Mercy Home ever since I first told her of their lives. My wife had given us some money to buy for them some sports equipment. We had hoped to bring the articles with us, but because winter was in full swing in Maine none of the sporting goods stores we went too had as yet gotten in their summer equipment. We were looking for soccer balls and volley balls and badminton sets (a favorite game in India). Because we couldn't find them in Maine, Coleen asked Marnie and me to find them in Kerala.

Shortly after one o'clock, we headed into Kottayam for an afternoon of shopping. The Simon's had a number of earrings to run for the graduation, so we hitched a ride. Again Binu was our driver for the trip into the big city. (To give you some idea on just how difficult shopping is in India; we went only 43 miles and made only 8 stops and it took us SIX hours to finish our list!) Our first stop was at the bank (South India National Bank) to get some cash; few places in Kerala take credit cards. Because we had missed lunch, our second stop was a restaurant. This eating place was the first one I had visited in India the year before. Marnie had a traditional India meal with the rest, while 'little sipe' and I had fish and chips (French fries) topped off with ice cream; Joshua's favorite food group, and Binu and Marnie shared a banana split!

Our third stop was at a sporting goods store, and I hope you are not picturing something like Dick's in your mind. In a back alley next to a variety of other small shops was a small room filled to the rafters with a variety of sporting equipment; Indian sporting equipment! No baseball bats, golfing equipment, basketballs, footballs, or anything that would even look like our American games. Within a short time Marnie and I had bought 6 badminton bats with a tube of birds and badminton net. The net could also be used for another favorite game in India: volleyball, so we bought a volley ball. We also bought a soccer ball; they call it football there, and three tennis like balls that they could use to play their most favorite sport: cricket! For the kids who didn't like outdoor sports, we also bought a chess set (another favorite India game) and a cram-board and pieces, a game I use to play as a child, and the whole lot cost less than $50!

With our presents for the orphans purchased, we would have to wait until Sunday to give them, but that is another story. The joy of buying for those who have so little is a pleasure that only those who have so much can appreciate, and all because of the simple gift of a wife and mother. After we had the new games for the children of the orphanage safety stored in Shibu's car, we moved on through the busy streets of Kottayam to a cloth store.

Again I wanted Marnie to witness the variety of materials available to those who make the colorful churidhars and chiffon sarees that Marnie had bought shortly after we arrived in Edyappara. After a few pictures and a walk around the three-floors of fabric, we walked around the corner to a gift store I had also visited on my first trip. There we bought some thank you cards (India style) and some graduation cards and a couple of wooden bowls for Coleen and of course Marnie had to buy a wooden elephant for herself. (Like father, like daughter!)

Our next stop was at a Christian Book Store were Shibu was going to buy a study Bible for each of the three graduates. He would buy two English Bibles and one Malayalam Bible, but as we waited for the clerk to find exactly what Shibu wanted, I made an interesting observation.

Shibu's Julie had spent over seven years in the United States and had gotten use to shopping at Wal-Mart. Julie, like her son, is more American than Indian in so many ways. If truth be told she is far more comfortable in the Good Old USA than in Kerala. One of the frustrations of knowing a better way is living outside that way! Shopping in India is so complicated and time consuming; while the Wal-Mart of America has spoiled us in getting what we need, or want quickly! I don't know how many times Julie would say, "If only there was a Wal-Mart here!"

As I looked through the book shelves for an interesting title, I came across a book that looked entertaining, but when I opened it up to see the contents and the price; what did I see? A Wal-Mart sticker! Wal-Mart's recycled books are finding there way to the bookstores of southern India. When I showed Julie the seal a faint smile came to her Indian face.

After the bookstore, we traveled to the 'wal-mart' of Kerala, called 'the G-Mart.' This variety store was another familiar place for me. We had shopped there a couple of times on my last trip. This is where we would buy the Indian spices for Coleen and I would get my Urbans Salted Cashews, the best in the world! It was here I also brought a Snickers bar for each of the members of our shopping team. One of my favorite pictures of the whole trip is a photograph of Abigail Simon with Snicker's bar in hand and chocolate all over her beautiful brown face!

Our eighth and final stop was in Karukachal where we picked up Marnie's homemade orange blouse to go with her fancy saree, her graduation outfit. Tomorrow would be graduation day at Kerala Baptist Bible College, and Marnie and I were now officially ready to blend into the surroundings and participate as Indians!

19

Agape Missions of India

II John 5— . . . that which we had from the beginning, that we love one another.

GRADUATION DAY had arrived and with it a series of events that only made this special day more special.

Last chapel took up most of our morning as the graduates, students, and staff of KBBC shared their last service together. I was once again honored to give the challenge. I spoke on the "Three D's for All Timothy's' (three male graduates): a doctrine we must believe, a discipline we must behave, and a dynamic we must burn; taken from II Timothy 1. Also among the events of the chapel was a farewell to Reneeshya, the college librarian. Her four-year responsibility was over, and she would soon be married and off to Assam to be a missionary with her husband. Many spoke of the joys they had together, but their pride of sending Reneeshya off to the mission field came across with much love. Tears were shed, gifts were given, and pictures were taken. Marnie gave Renee our gift and hugged her and cried. (They had become like sisters in their short time together.) Then Reneeshya gave a very emotional testimony; then in typical Indian style we had a brown-bag luncheon.

That afternoon I was off with Shaju, his son Jerry, and our driver Bijew to visit my dear Indian friend Johnson Matthews. Johnson had been my translator for the evangelistic meetings I had the year before at the Annual Convention of the IGBC. Next to Shibu and Julie, Johnson has the best English in Kerala, so I was able to get to know him and his ministry quite well. On my 'to-do' list for my second trip to Edyappara was to visit Johnson's mission at Kumpanthanam.

We traveled the five miles to the Agape Mission in Shaju's 'Glenna girl': the name I gave my grandmother's 1982 Olds Omega that had been given to me by my 95 year old grammie. Shaju's old Ambassador car had been given to him by his father. Waiting for us when we arrived was Johnson, his wife Lydia, eight orphans from the Agape Children's Home, his parents, and a few members of the Kumpanthanam Baptist Church. As with all Indian welcomes, I was greeted like the long-lost friend who finally came for a visit. It was my first visit, but I felt like an old visitor. The greetings were friendly and refreshing, seeing I had only meet Johnson once before. We were shown around the compound (including the only baptistery I have seen in India), introduced to everybody (four of the orphans were still at school), and of course treated to a fruity lunch.

After the formal greeting, Johnson, Shaju, and I went into a room to talk privately. I had come on a mission; I had a gift. Just before I left for India I had prayed that I might have some money to give to the Agape Mission. All my funds were designated, so in prayer I asked for a special gift. The very next day in the mail came a check for $500 from a couple I only knew through some friends at my church, but for me it was Johnson's money. As I handed over the money and told the story of how it came, Johnson realized how God could meet his needs through strangers from America.

I only spent a few hours with Johnson Matthews on my first trip to Kangazha, and most of them while preaching God's Word at the Edyappara crusade while he interpreted my English into Malayalam. My second trip to Kerala also only allowed me to spend a couple of hours with this dedicated servant of Christ, but this time I saw him in a different light; enough for me to conclude that he might just be a 'George Muller.' If Joy Thomas is the Paul of Orissa; then Johnson Matthews is the George Muller of Kumpanthanam.

Johnson Matthews is a man in his early 40's. Born to Matthew and Mary of Kumpanthanam (I got to meet them and visit their home next door to the mission), Johnson left home as a single man and for many years worked alone as a missionary in two northern states of India. In the early 1990s, Johnson returned to Kerala to pastor a church about twenty miles from his folk's home. It was during this time he married his lovely wife Lydia; they are still praying for children, pray with them, for children in India are see as the greatest blessing of the Lord! In 2000, Johnson returned home to care for his aging parents (not because he was the youngest son, the traditional duty of Kerala children, but because he was their only child), and decided to start the Agape Mission.

With no money Johnson Matthews prayed, and the Lord began the work. While translating for a pastor from Virginia, he was asked his heart's desire? Johnson told his dream of starting a 'mission' next door to his parent's home. There was already a building there, but over the years a bad relationship had formed between the neighbors. The Virginia preacher told Johnson to go next door and ask the neighbors if they were willing to sell their house and property. Despite his doubts and reservations, Johnson did as the preacher had asked. To his surprise the family said yes, and the man from Virginia was able to raise the money back in the USA and the Agape Mission was born.

Six years later it has developed into the Agape Children's Home and the Kumpanthanam Baptist Church. Besides Johnson's responsibilities as pastor and director of the home, he visits and has services in nine local jails each month. Every Saturday night the church conducts evangelistic meetings somewhere in the area. They also conduct youth meetings and numerous prayer meetings and Bible studies during the week. When I arrived they were having their weekly Friday fast. (I must admit I wondered whether they were having it for prayer reasons, or just to conserve food, yet they feed us), and they also have a VBS and an annual evangelistic crusade at the church.

Men like Johnson Matthews put me to shame when it comes to spiritual work because they do it all depending on God and God alone for their support. George would be proud! The morning I spend with the dear saints at Kumpanthanam was an inspiring addition to the chapel service at KBBC, how could the graduation top that?

20

An Indian Princess Gets Ready for Graduation

Lamentations 1:1— . . . princess among the provinces . . .

AFTER I returned from my visit with Johnson Matthews and his ministry, the rest of the afternoon and early evening was given to preparation for graduation, the primary reason Marnie and I had been invited to India. Little did Marnie dream of the special part she would play in this very unique college graduation celebration.

I had bought Marnie a special Indian outfit to wear to graduation, and upon my return form Kumpanthanam I found Reneeshya and Julie turning my all-American girl into a Kerala princess. I wish I had the words to describe the process it takes to get a chiffon sari on. As I watched the transformation, it was hard to believe the details Indian women put into their clothing. Despite the primitive conditions, the Kerala women always seem to be dressed in their Sunday-best, but on special occasions, like a college graduation, they take it a step further. For in addition to the sari, there is the gold jewelry they add. Julie was kind enough to share with Marnie all the extras she needed to make the dress standout; to make her into a princess, and Marnie would tell you to this day that she felt like a princess in that orange and blue sari. And if she felt like one, it was nothing to how she was treated when she finally stepped out into the courtyard of the Kerala Baptist Bible College campus and to all her waiting fans.

Was it her auburn hair; her white skin against the bright colors of her sari? Within seconds Marnie was surrounded by every young man on campus. Everybody wanted a picture with this new Indian princess; as Marnie would say it was embarrassing the attention she was being given. The three KBBC graduates were also there, but I dare say there were more pictures taken of Marnie than them. It might have been the uniqueness of the situation, but for my daughter it was a night of being the center of attention. Shibu even had to come from the church and order the students to stop taking pictures and gather at the courtyard of the Kangazha Church where all the official pictures were to be taken. My daughter had disrupted the flow of events!

Even when we got to the church the demands for pictures taken with my daughter didn't stop. It was as if Marnie had suddenly appeared and this beauty queen was the hit of the ball. Marnie would have nothing formally to do during graduation, but the KBBC graduation ceremony of 2007 will forever be remembered as the event when an American girl turned Indian princess turned the heads of every Youngman in Edyappara. I watched from afar knowing the joy this was bringing to my daughter's heart. Marnie was once again apart of a foreign culture; she felt accepted in that culture, and for an evening in a strange land she was seen as one of them; something Marnie had desired since she was 8! (One of the reasons I wanted to bring Marnie on this trip to India was to show her that the bitter experience she had in Eastern Europe was not the norm. I wanted her to regain that passion for missions she had lost. To this day she will tell you that India relit the flame in her soul for missions that have yet to be extinguished!)

As I watched Marnie around the graduates, I remembered something that had happened earlier in our trip with another Indian princess:

It was the morning Marnie and I had gone over to the orphanage to play with the kids and to take their pictures. As we walked back to the college, we stopped at the new land (where the Hindu house had been located) and watched as the young men from the college cleaned and cleared the lot. Bijoy, Jaldev, and Billy were cutting down the bushes and small trees that had grown up since the property had been abandoned. It was well over 100 degrees as they cut and burned and raked. They had been at it for nearly four hours as we talked with them of what was left to do. As we watched, they showed us the cardamom vines, the pepper bushes, the coffee tress, and the coco plants located between the new land and Annamma's house. After a few more minutes, the call for lunch was sounded; it was one o'clock in the afternoon.

When we arrived at Annamma's house, the small dwelling was full of people. Marnie and I didn't know it at the time, but we were about to experience another interesting twist in Malayalam culture: the home going of an Indian baby girl. I was surprised to see Monsee, Shiela husband (Shibu and Shaju's other sister), there with his father and a lady he introduced as his cousin. It was then Marnie and I discovered that ever since Shiela and Monsee's second daughter had been born both Shiela and Lydia had been staying with Annamma. It is a custom of that region for the new born to stay in the grandparent's house for three-months after the birth. Then it is a very special day when the father comes (usually with other members of the family, why Monsee's dad and cousin were there) to get his wife and child. Marnie and I participated in Lydia's home going following the special noon meal.

I had meet Monsee and Shiela and their first daughter, Libby, on my first trip to Kerala. I had especially liked Monsee, a teacher during the week and an evangelist on weekends. He spoke very good English, so I was able to have meaningful conversations with him. He is of the Brethren faith and an Elder in his church, for which I learned on that Saturday afternoon that his father was the chief Elder of their church. I had also learned that in both of my trips that denominationalism isn't as hostile as it is in America which was very refreshing to me. But I did and still do have issue with some of the customs of these people. Don't get me wrong, these people are very content in their lifestyle and their way of doing things, but as for me, I would have had a hard time with my daughter Marnie living in her Nana's (what Marnie calls her grandmother) house for the first three-months of her life, especially if I was living somewhere else!

Monsee had hired a private car to take his princess home in, and as they left the tears flowed as if they would never see each other again. That is why I have cherished every moment I have been able to spend with my princess, and our trip to India did include some of the greatest moments of all, and to witness again Marnie's love for missions (the reason she is at Dallas Theological today) was a bonus of this my second trip to Kerala .

21

A Three-fold Cord

Ecclesiastes 4:12— . . . a threefold cord is not quickly broken.

FROM 5:30 to 7:00 PM, Marnie and I mingled with the staff and students and invited guests of KBBC in the courtyard of the Kangazha Church. Countless pictures were taken of my daughter in her orange sari and of me in my pink (yes, pink) CAP AND ROBE. My first college graduation since my own in 1973 will never be forgotten because of the gown I had to wear. Shibu failed to tell me until the day before the event just what my attire would be. Once I saw it, I knew why he had failed to share that vital piece of information. I was quite the sight!

We marched in at 7:00 PM and marched out at a little after 9:00 PM. The program included a prayer by Professor Bobby Kuriakose; scripture reading by Professor Raju Sagar and Professor Joji Matthew; the academic report by Professor Sabu Andrews; a prayer of dedication by Professor Matthew Kodithottam, and the closing prayer by Professor Joseph Daniel. The Simon family was well represented with Shibu giving the welcome and conferring the degrees, and his brother Shaju sharing the announcements.

Their mother Annamma gave out the gifts, and the IGBC choir had the special music. The congregation sang two familiar English hymns: To God Be The Glory and Onward Christian Soldiers; no they didn't know the theme of my charge! The church was very, very hot and that pink (Oh, did I tell you it was made of heavy wool!) robe only made it hotter as I stood to speak. But I wouldn't have missed this experience for the world. With my daughter watching, it was one of those events in a person's life that will never, ever be forgotten!

Because the graduating class of 2007 at KBBC was three young men, I decided to challenge them with the precept of Solomon printed above. I also thought I would use the story of David's three valiant soldiers, Adino, Eleazer, and Shammah, and their quest to get David a drink of water from a Bethlehem well (II Samuel 23:13–17) to illustrate this classic Biblical concept. My theme was on volunteerism and what it takes to be a soldier in Christ's army. I also sang for them W. S. Brown's old church hymn, "A call for loyal soldiers comes to one and all; soldiers for the conflict, will you heed the call? Will you answer quickly, with a ready cheer; will you be enlisted as a volunteer?" I shared with them the three characteristics that make a three-fold cord unbreakable:

1. First, *You Must Have Loytalty*. II Samuel 23:13. Located near his hometown, David's first and most famous stronghold was in the Cave of Adullam (I Samuel 22:1 and Psalms 142). It was harvest time and very hot (as it was in Kerala that day) as David dreamed out loud of the sweet, cooling waters of the well at Bethlehem. Despite the fact that this was no

order, just a desire, the three mighty men still left the safety of their stronghold for the danger of the mission. So too are we to be such soldiers for Christ (II Timothy 2:3–4)! But why did these three warriors have such loyalty for David; that would cause them to risk their lives for him?

2. Second, *You Must Have Charity*. II Samuel 23:14–15. Only one emotion could cause three men to fight their way through the valley of giants (Rephaim, and the Philistines were known for having giants in their army) to an occupied, fortified town for a cup of water: Love! We sing, "Oh, How I Love Jesus", but do we really? How far are we ready to go to please our Captain (Hebrews 2:10)? There was not only love here for David, but there was love of one another as well (John 15:13). Most soldiers will tell you that when they are in the midst of a bitter battle very few think of family, or nation, but that in the end they fight for their buddy beside them. These three men loved David, but as they fought their way back to Adullam they were fighting for the survival of each other! And so must we fight the 'good fight of faith.'

3. Third, *You Must Have Unity*. II Samuel 23:16–17. The battle at the well at Bethlehem was won because of 'oneness.' They were one in purpose and plan and protection. Side by side, back to back, they fought their way into Bethlehem, fought while getting that precious cup of water, and fought their way back to David (Philippians 2:2). If there is an attribute that is missing among most Christians today it is the char-

> acteristic of unity. Oh, what we could accomplish for our Lord, if only we as fellow soldiers were unified. These qualities were found in the four friends that brought the palsy man to Jesus (Mark 2). Are these found in you? Go forth a loyal soldier, a loving volunteer, a united three-fold cord!

After the graduation we gathered with the families of the graduates and their friends for a set-down meal. During my first visit in India, I had stayed faithful to my Western ways of eating. Marnie on the other hand had other ideas for her American father. Almost from her first meal in Kerala, Marnie had adapted to the Indian style of eating with her fingers. I had practiced a few times at the Simon's, but I had yet to eat with my fingers in public. I find the practice very uncomfortable and strange, but as Marnie and I sat down at the head table waiting our graduation meal I noticed for the first time there was no silver ware by my plate. Annamma had always brought along Western knives and forks and spoons whenever I eat outside her home. In her home I was treated like a westerner, and was never asked to eat with my fingers. It seemed somebody had forgotten in all the excitement of graduation, or was it time for me to step outside my comfort zone and adopt a new way of eating?

With Marnie's help and a smile on the face of the graduation guests, I for the first time eat a meal in public with my fingers, perhaps for the first time since I was a baby! I had certainly watched enough people do it so I understood how, but it still felt odd to me. Nevertheless, once the meal was over and Marnie and I went outside to wash our hands, I did feel that I had overcome another obstacle of being a Kerala Indian. Now if I could only take my shoes off when entering a home or church!

22

Seven for Soneeta

Job 30:22— . . . Thou causest me to ride upon it . . .

WE LEFT Edyappara around 7:45 AM for the elephant training center at Kobanadu. The seventy plus mile trek took us three hours north of Kangazha through countless towns, villages, and cities of central Kerala. Along for the ride was Shibu, Julie, Joshua, Abigail, and of course ,Binu was our driver. Professor Bobbi was also with us when we left. We were taking him home after the busy academic year, and we dropped him off about a half an hour from the center. By 10:45 AM, we were driving into the lane leading to the grounds, and there before us was the largest elephant I had ever seen coming straight at us in the middle of the road.

What excited Marnie and I most about this huge elephant in the middle of the road was the fact that there were people on its back (we would learn later 'her' back). I quickly asked, "Can we ride the elephant?" My last up close and personal experience with an Indian elephant was just a few short minute on the back of one for a few quick pictures. I had never yet actually ridden an elephant! After touring Thekkadi the year before, we found a man beside the road in Kumily renting out his elephant for photo shoots for tourists. I got my picture taken on the back of 'Maria', but no ride. For my second trip to India, I wanted my daughter and me to take an actual ride on an elephant, and it looked like we had come to the right place to do just that!

Once we got by the elephant and through the gate, I quickly paid 400 rupies (not even ten dollars) for all seven of us to ride the elephant we had seen. As we waited for the elephant to return from the trip it was on, we learned that this elephant was called 'Soneeta', and that she was a 37-year old work elephant. She had been retired to the center and now spent her days giving tourists like us rides. We also learned that despite living in India most of their lives neither Shibu or Julie or Binu had ridden an elephant either, and of course the young kids hadn't! This was going to be the first ride for all seven of us. The year before I had tried to get Joshua to set on the elephant with me, but he refused, but this time the first ride would be taken by Marnie and me and little sipe.

We climbed the ramp up to Soneeta's back. (This elephant was so tall that an airplane ramp had to be used just to get onto her back.) Unlike 'Marie', Soneeta had no saddle; we were going to ride our first elephant bareback! Marnie was the first to swing her legs (we had taken off our shoes) around Soneeta's neck. There was a large rope around the elephant's neck, something for Marnie to hang on too. Then I put Joshua behind Marnie before I climbed on board. I grabbed the ends of the rope that was wrapped around Soneeta's neck, and then we were off. We quickly discovered that elephants have porcupine-like hair all over their body. These hairs are very sharp until you push them down. We also discovered that under that hair was a very slippery hide. With each step Soneeta took, we felt like we were going to slip off. The twenty-minute ride was a thrill beyond description, and then to watch Shibu, Julie, Abigail, and Binu repeat the ride was even more exciting. I wish I could show you all the pictures!

After we rode Soneeta, I thought our Saturday at the Kobanadu Elephant Rescue Center had reached its zenith; how wrong I was, for we were just getting started. It wasn't long into my life that I learned from my father that it isn't so much what you know that counts, but who you know!

A phone call from a friend of Shibu's in Edyappara was going to change our status as just another tourist to VIP treatment. Shibu's friend had retired from the center just the year before, so he still had plenty of contacts at Kobanadu. Once our elephant ride was over, we were ushered to a place in the park where even the native Indians were not allowed to go. At first we didn't understand this as we made out way under the ropes that separated the public part of the park from the private (staff only) part of the park. Once on the other side of the fence, we came to a huge timber structure. This corral had once been used to enclose wild elephants (it is now illegal in India to capture wild elephants) before their training began; now it was a nursery!

I had seen wild elephants and working elephants on my first trip to Kerala, but all those elephants had been mature 'annas' (Malayalam for elephant). Now Marnie and I were going to get to see and touch baby elephants. There were two baby elephants in the compound the day we were there: a five-month old and a nine-month old. I walked up to the nine-month old and immediately she came over to me. Her small trunk began to touch my face. What a thrill to feel the cold nose of that young elephant on my hot face (it was nearing midday and the temperature was well over 100 with a very high humidity). Marnie took pictures as the little (she probably did not stand more than three feet high) elephant stuck her head out through the foot thick planks. Then, for me, perhaps the most meaningful event of the entire day took place. 'Parabha' (I found out later that was her name) placed the tip of her little trunk squarely on the tip of my nose. I had been kissed by a baby elephant!

As we left the nursery area, I decided to call my new friend 'parable'; because that is how her Malayalam name sounded to me. Soon it was 'parable' this and 'parable' that. I was thrilled, that is until Shibu asked, "Why are you calling that elephant 'parable'?" Once I explained, he set me straight, and I wished I had never heard the truth, for I soon discovered that I had actually been kissed by a Hindu goddess. Come to find out the little elephant (Hindus worship elephants as one of their gods) had been named after the wife of the third person of the Hindu trinity. Parabha was a Hindu goddess, and I had been loved by a 'god'! At first this brought a sour taste to my mouth, but after awhile I began to realize despite the truth, or fable, I had experienced a marvel in nature that few have had the privilege to enjoy. I am now proud of the fact that I have been kissed by a baby 'anna', Indian goddess or not!

23

Playing with Elephants

Job 40:20— . . . Where all the beasts of the field play.

After eleven very busy days (sometimes three meetings a day) of travel and ministry, Marnie and I were ready for our one day in India to play tourist. Shibu had arranged for us to visit an old elephant training ground that had been converted over to an animal rescue center. However, before we could head for Kobanadu, we had to answer a phone call!

Cancer calls have now become a common ingredient in my life. These are the calls you never forget despite the passing of time. I still remember that Thursday call from Washburn informing us of my father-in-law's cancer (lung and liver cancer that would take him within 15 months). It had also just been two years since we were informed that my dear wife had breast cancer, a cancer that almost stopped my first trip to India in 2006. Before, in between, and since, other calls have come informing me of cancer in the members of my flock. None are easy, but when you are over nine thousand miles away it adds another dimension to the word 'cancer.'

I was up at six o'clock dreaming of the trip my daughter and I was going to take to visit a group of elephants. During my 40-day stay in 2006, I had only one tourist day in my busy schedule. That year the Simon family took me to Thekkadi to see wild elephants in a national preserve; it was and still is the best personal day I have spent in that grand land. We were not going back to Thekkadi, but we were going to a place I had heard about and almost got to go on my first trip: Kobanadu. I had actually met a man who worked at the Kobanadu Elephant Rescue Center, but because of a motorcycle accident he couldn't take me that year. He promised me if I returned that he would get me in, and now I was ready, but less than an hour before we were to leave the phone rang, and I heard Marnie say from the living room, "Bubby, (her name for me) you need to talk to mother!"

For nearly two years my mother-in-law, Opal Meister, had been complaining to various doctors of a pain in her side. She had also complained that no matter what she ate it ran straight through her. Finally after we got her settled in Ellsworth; she had moved from northern Maine to coastal Maine just before Thanksgiving 2006, we found a doctor who took her seriously. Many tests had been run and one of the last was to check her colon; that exam revealed a large cancerous tumor. She was to be operated on the very day Marnie and I would get back from India. Despite the shock and the fact we were so far away, both Marnie and I were at peace that the Good Lord would watch over Opal and Coleen until we returned. (The operation by the way went well. The doctor was able to get the entire tumor, and it was revealed that it hadn't spread. At the writing of this book

Opal is fully recovered with no cancer returning in the last two years! Praise The Lord!)

Whether good news from a far country (Proverbs 25:25) or bad news, Jesus is able to deal with all situations and balance the bad news with a great blessing! For during my first 40-days in India, I only saw 8 elephants. In my ten-days up until the call about Opal's cancer, Marnie and I had already seen ten elephants. Little did we know that after riding an elephant, and touching and loving two baby elephants at Kobanadu Elephant Rescue Center, we were going to be allowed to play with the elephants!

Once again to our surprise Marnie and I and the Simon family were lead into a compound just around the corner from the nursery where four elephants were cared for. Once again we watched as the rest of the visitors to the center were kept behind a rock wall while we were given a personal tour of this section of the park. Here we were able to actually walk up to the elephants and touch them and have our pictures taken with them. We were introduced to 'Echo' and "Eve', two four-year old females. There were also two two-year old elephants behind them feeding, but it would be with Echo and Eve that we would play.

As we stood to the side of Eve, the handler asked Marnie to stand in front of her. He placed a bunch of artificial flowers in the trunk of Eve, and then asked Marnie to reach our hand toward the elephant. When she did Eve gave Marnie the flowers. It was then I realized that we were putting on a show for the visitors to the center. People laughed and smiled as Eve repeated the demonstration to me. I couldn't believe that we were being given such access to these special creatures. In what American zoo would Marnie and I be given such a privileged play time?

After Eve, we were off to meet Echo, where once again I was asked to stand before the five-foot high beast. This time I was asked to bow before the elephant as the trainer put a myla (a flowery stringer of garland, the traditional Malayalam welcome symbol) in Echo's trunk. When I bowed before Echo, she placed the myla around my neck. Echo repeated the trick for Marnie. Once again we had a grand time playing with these elephants and enjoying volunteering for their show. After this we were off to meet the biggest male elephant in the park.

Down near Big River was a shed that had two rooms. The first room was filled and I mean filled with Soneeta, the elephant we had ridden that morning when we first came to the center. She was on a break from her transportation duties, and eating her lunch. Next to her, and not quite as big, was a 12-year old male named 'Leelagerdon.' As we neared his cage, his trainer motioned for us to come inside. What impressed us about this elephant were his huge tusks. As Marnie got nearer, the handler asked Marnie to stand under the elephant and hold up his tusks. When she did the elephant raised his head. With her arms fully extended, Marnie stood under this massive creature. Marnie would admit afterwards there was some fear playing with elephants!

After a walk in the Big River to cool down, we made the long trip home to Edyappara. Despite the news that had greeted us earlier that morning, our heavenly Father had in His great timing blended bad news with a blessed experience, so that in my memory that day will not just be known for a cancer call!

24

Jasmine and Roses

Isaiah 28:4—And the glorious beauty,
which is on the head of the fat valley,
shall be a fading flower . . .

OUR LAST Sunday in India found Marnie and me heading for the church at Ayroor, my 17th church visit, with Shibu and Binu. This was the third church planted by Brother Simon, behind Kangazha and Poovanmala. Pastor V P Joseph greeted us as did his congregation after we climbed another Kerala hill. The temperature was already over 100 by mid-morning, but the refreshing fellowship was worth the effort.

Our mylas were made out of fresh jasmine and roses, the most beautiful and best smelling of all I had ever received; Marnie agreed! They also had fresh coconut milk for us to drink; which we both enjoyed. We had a typical Indian morning worship service with plenty of singing and praying. Marnie gave her testimony again, and I spoke on "The Prodigal Came . . ." from Luke 15:11–24. It was a pleasant morning with God's people in the hills of Kerala about 12 miles from Edyappara.

On our way back to Kangazha we stopped at Poovanmala, the very first church plant I visited in 2006. The whole church congregation was all still there to greet us as we drove into the church yard early that afternoon. It was like I had never left. We meet old friends and made new ones. We got back to Annamma's house around 2 o'clock. There waiting in the yard was Binu's mother and Jacob (our auto driver) John's mother. Marnie placed a myla of jasmine and roses around their necks. We knew they wouldn't last, and we wanted others to enjoy their beauty and fragrance; besides, Marnie had fallen in love with these two ladies, as they had with her. Then we had a lunch of chicken soup, fried potatoes, and for dessert, Julie's fruit cake.

Later that afternoon we went to the orphanage to give the kids our 'game' gifts. Marnie shared the story of Jonah, and then we presented the sporting equipment. I can't explain or describe the expressions on those kids' faces as we tried to get them to understand that these articles were now theirs. Despite the 100 degree plus weather, we then went outside and played with the children and took pictures with their new toys. As I kicked the soccer ball around and watched them play, all I could think about was the artificial flowers and drawings and carved birds they had given us. In our attempt to give to them, they in their own sweet way gave back to us so much more!

That evening at the Kangazha Church, we were the honored guests at our farewell service? Marnie shared her 14th and last message in Kerala on "My Blessing from India" taken from Ephesians 1:3. I shared my 21st and last message on "Jesus Sat Down" taken from Hebrews 1:3. Afterward, Marnie and I gave our gifts to the Simon Family (earrings from my wife, LL Bean flashlights from my mother-in-law, and three gold rings Brother Simon had given me nearly eight years before. I gave them back to Annamma from her late husband; she was touched!). In turn we were given gifts, for you can never out give these people. It was certainly a jasmine and rose kind of day with God's people in Kerala, India.

Early that next morning I ventured out into the heat and humidity of Edyappara for one last walk into my Eden. I left Marnie sleeping as I exited the college compound turning left for downtown Edyappara. As I got to the bus stop, Bijew (the school bus driver) was turning the corner heading for Annamma's house to pick up his van. After a Malayalam greeting, I quickly turned right on the Salvation Army Road, but within a few hundred feet I turned left. My destination was a little valley I called Pineapple Hollow (because of the fields of pineapple planted there), one of the great sights of Edyappara. I had discovered this picturesque vale late in my first stay. Unlike the numerous other valleys in the area, this one was void of trees. In previous hikes, I had only strolled to the brow of the hill overlooking the valley, but this time I was determined to descend into the valley and climb the hill on the other side. (Interestingly, I have just returned from another trip to India. I also returned to this valley to show my deacon friend Russ Coffin its beauty. To my surprise in the three years since I was last there the owners of that valley have planted rubber tree on both sides of the hill blocking the marvelous view. Pineapple Hollow is now Rubber Tree Valley!)

The sun had made its way over the horizon to the east as I walked the small country road into the valley. The sweat was already flowing from all my pours as I greeted the early morning workers and residents along the lane. As

I climbed the other side I was surprised to see a familiar face, but who was she, where had I meet her? It was then the lady's husband appeared and to my surprise it was Pastor P C Matthew, Reggie's dad and pastor of the Poovanmala Church. It was always a surprise for me to learn just how far the ministers of Kerala travel to pastor their churches (nearly 20 miles for PC). Our conversation was blessed, but they were surprised that I was out walking in such hot weather. I explained it was my last walk into their beautiful valley, and it was my last wish to see it and enjoy it again, no matter the heat. As I worked my way back the way I came, I had one final stop to make before the heat drove me back in-doors to a cooling fan and shower.

Leaving Pineapple Hollow, I walked a small trail that lead me back to the mission compound. I had discovered the shortcut one morning as I was looking for cobras. (Which I have yet to find) The vine-covered lane brought me back to the Bethany School, and who was waiting for me when I emerged from the forest but Joy Thomas. Joy was heading into town for supplies, but all I could think was Shibu had sent out his spy to find me. I quickly said goodbye, and hurried off to my most favorite spot in Edyappara. I looked back to make sure Joy wasn't following, and turned left into my canopy-covered path. This rubber tree lined lane was still producing sap as I walked one last time through this pristine cathedral of wood-covered hills and rock walls. As I write this chapter, I have just looked over my left shoulder to a 20 by 36 inch blowup of a picture I took the first time I found that trail. It is my way of never forgetting the Eden I found in Kerala. 'The glorious beauty, which is on the head of the fat valley.'

Postlude

Sunset at Kovalam Beach

Joshua 1:4—And unto the great sea toward the going down of the sun . . .

After my last walk to my favorite spots in Edyappara, Marnie and I started the very difficult process of saying goodbye to our Kerala family. Even before we could venture out, our friends were stopping by. Annamma's brother's family brought Marnie an Indian wooden tray. The night before Binu's mother had given Marnie a beautiful pin in the shape of India. Shibu gave me a letter he had translated from Malayalam from the folks at Venmony. Julie gave me a prayer shawl for Coleen, and Binu brought Marnie Kerala flowers! Our bags had to be repacked.

Just before we left town, Marnie had one final stop she wanted to make. She had to say goodbye to Jason, Professor Andrew's little boy. We walked across the street to the college, and found the small lad playing in the courtyard. As he did from the beginning, the minute he saw Marnie he ran into her arms, and they hugged and kissed. Marnie had become attached to Jason and the Kerala people, as they had become attached to her. Tears flowed as we left Annamma's yard for the 100 mile drive to Trivandrum. The trip was coming to an end far too quickly, both for me and my daughter. Only the Good Lord knows the reason we have made these contacts and developed these relationships. (When we got home Marnie would be formally invited back to teach at KBBC for three months in 2008. That experience convinced Marnie that a ministry of teaching was her calling, the reason she is at Dallas Theological Seminary getting her masters. Now I know why "Though *One* Go With Me.") I was changed during my first trip to India, and Marnie was changed in her first trip as well!

Four hours later we were at the Moonstar Motel checking into our over night room; that is after we got stuck in the elevator because our bags and our friends were too heavy for the elevator to lift! We were in a hurry because we still had 17 miles to travel to fulfill Marnie's last desire for this trip. Marnie loves the ocean, any ocean, and she wanted to dip her feet in the Indian Ocean before we headed home. She also loves sunsets, and she wanted to see the sun set over the Indian Ocean. I had told her of my adventure in the Indian Ocean the year before, and she wanted to experience the thrill for herself. Binu somehow managed to weave our way through rush hour traffic, for by a little after five o'clock we were standing in the sands of Kovalam Beach.

For the next hour and a half, I watched Shibu, Shaju, Binu, Joshua, and Marnie play like children in the heavy surf. The boys had brought me to the same beach a little over a year before, but there was something different about this time. I saw a family at play; swimming, body surfing, building sand castles, buying roasted peanuts from the beach vendors, and watching a spectacular Indian sunset over Kovalam Cove. Marnie and Binu were like best friends as they created Edyappara in the sands of Kovalam. I walked from one end of the beach to the other enjoying the refreshing and much cooler air, the best of the trip. I took pictures and prayed that this wasn't my last trip to Kerala (and it wasn't for I would return in 2010). I had fallen in love with this place and its people all over again.

As the hot sun dipped into the Indian Ocean, we watched in amazement at one of the great sights of nature took place before our eyes. Whether the coast of Maine, or the coast of Kerala, a sunset isn't an ending, but just an anticipation of another day spent with family and friends.

We left Kovalam Beach shortly after that wonderful sunset. On the way back to Trivandrum, we stopped for take-out, Indian style. We ate supper at Sheena and Joe's house (Shibu and Shaju's sister) before heading back to the Moonstar Motel for a short night's sleep because we had to be at the airport by four AM.

I will never forget my 56th birthday for as long as I live. Most of my birthdays have come and gone without any meaningful event worth remembering; not so my March 6, 2007 birthday (for one thing it would last 34 1\2 hours). I was up at 2:30 AM after only four hours rest. Marnie changed back into her American cloths, and we repacked for the last time. The 'boys' picked us up around 3:30 AM and we headed into the quiet, empty (the only time of the day I have ever seen the streets of India both quiet and empty) streets of Trivandrum for our ten minute ride to the airport, located just outside of town. It was only fitting that on our way we saw out 19th elephant of the trip: a huge male swaying slowly in a dark lot near a work site; it was the only birthday present I needed.

We arrived at the Trivandrum Airport just before four. It was then the tears started to flow again. Binu and Marnie hugged and cried as if they would never see each other again (they would within ten-months). We shook hands and prayed and left our dear friends standing on the street (only passengers are allowed in Indian airports). Without any difficulty, Marnie and I made our way through the series of check points to our gate, and by five we were boarding our plane for Kuwait City.

Each of the legs of our flight home was long and tiring, and with each stop I simply prayed that I might be back in Maine before my birthday ended. Because there is a ten and a half hour difference between the east coast of the United States and the State of Kerala, I hoped there was enough time to travel the 9000 miles. From Kuwait City we traveled to London, and from London we flew to New York. Because we were supposed to get in around 5:30 PM, we thought we might be able to get an earlier flight into Portland. We touched down at JFK at six, and without much trouble we went through customs, got our three bags, and passed through immigration in double quick time. We were ahead of schedule, and all we had left was to take the Air Train to the Delta Terminal and catch an early flight home, or so we thought.

When we got to the ticket counter we discovered there were was no early flights, we had missed the last one by just half an hour, so I spent 5 hours of my 56th birthday at JFK, but I was still with family! We finally boarded a plane for Maine at 10:50 PM, and as the clock ticked into March 7th, we made a successful landing at the Portland Jetport. We still had a three hour car ride home, but there waiting for us (because Coleen was with her mother waiting her cancer operation) were Greg and Karen Bowden, dear friends from our church in Ellsworth; a fitting birthday present. My last lesson from India was to realize I have always had good friends waiting for me on both ends of my travels, and the sun had set on another great adventure to a far off and distant place with my daughter. It is my dream and desire that we might be able to do it again, and relive "Though One Go with Me."

(Postscript: If everything goes according to plan in May of 2010 Marnie and I will be on a plane together for Israel where we will participate in a study tour of the Holy Land through Dallas Theological Seminary! A journey I hope to share with you in another book, a fitting addition to our Paris and India adventures.)

Barry Blackstone
April 11, 2007

www.ingramcontent.com/pod-product-compliance
Lightning Source LLC
Chambersburg PA
CBHW070609310726
48982CB00001B/30

* 9 7 8 1 4 9 8 2 5 7 0 6 0 *